Strong hands grasped Denise's shoulders, steadying her. The familiar scent of cologne revealed the unexpected caller.

"Jaden, what are you doing here?" She looked up into the dark brown eyes that shimmered with a sexy glint. Their power sucked her body into a limp mass; she stepped closer. Her hands were plastered against his chest. Her fingers clawed at his shirt, one step ahead of her brain.

For the life of her, she had to concentrate on his words. All she saw were his full lips and flashes of his teeth.

"I want to kiss you," he breathed.

Denise swallowed. Guess he wasn't asking about her well-being.

"I want you, too."

Books by Michelle Monkou

Kimani Romance

Sweet Surrender
Here and Now
Straight to the Heart
No One but You
Gamble on Love

Kimani Arabesque

Open Your Heart
Finders Keepers
Give Love
Making Promises
Island Rendezvous

MICHELLE MONKOU

became a world traveler at three years old when she left her birthplace of London, England, and moved to Guyana, South America. She then moved to the United States as a young teen. She was an avid reader, which, mixed with her cultural experiences, set the tone for a vivid imagination. It wasn't long before the stories in her head became stories on paper.

In the middle of writing romances, she added a master's of international business to her bachelor's degree in English. Michelle was nominated for the 2003 Emma Award for Favorite New Author. She continues to write romances with complex characters and intricate plots. Visit her Web site for further information, and to sign up for her newsletter and contests, at http://www.michellemonkou.com.

Having lived on three continents, Michelle currently resides in the Washington, D.C., metropolitan area with her family. To contact her, write to P.O. Box 2904, Laurel, Maryland 20709, or e-mail her at michellemonkou@comcast.net.

GAMBLE ON

Love

MICHELLE MONKOU

THE LADIES of DISTINCTION

KIMANI
ROMANCE

To my sister authors: Celeste O. Norfleet and
Candice Poarch—always in my heart.

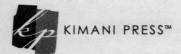

KIMANI PRESS™

ISBN-13: 978-0-373-86086-9
ISBN-10:   0-373-86086-2

GAMBLE ON LOVE

Dear Reader,

Step into the world of Xi Sigma Theta Sorority, Inc. Denise Dixon and her four sisters from the pledge line— the Ladies of Distinction—have forged a deep friendship. They have shared the trials and tribulations of their college years and now embark on finding their destiny as young professionals. Each soror will share her story of pain, redemption and, ultimately, love.

As a member of Sigma Gamma Rho Sorority, Inc., I wanted to create stories highlighting the tight bond among sorority sisters. African-American fraternal organizations have had a long history of servicing our communities, forming powerful networks and working with our youth. As we cut our affiliation from the few that have negative and hurtful intentions, I look forward to focused and unified messages from the various Greek organizations in the twenty-first century.

If you are a member of a sorority or enjoy a close-knit group of dear friends, share your positive experiences in building on sisterhood beyond the family. I have had many great friends throughout my life and I look forward to forging more friendships in the future.

Contact me at michellemonkou@comcast.net.

Blessings,

Michelle Monkou

Chapter 1

Fresh from a fifty-minute session with her personal trainer, Denise Dixon drove into the small city of Bloomsburg, an hour north of Chicago. It was a Friday afternoon, on the cusp of dusk, and the roads were jammed with professionals escaping the hectic madness of the Windy City. The sidewalks and walking paths were filled with joggers and speed walkers and every other person appeared to have a dog attached to a leash out for their daily routine.

Daily exercise was her therapy. One hundred fifty dollars an hour for her troubles seemed a bit over-priced. But that was her cross to bear.

Denise turned right at a corner by a church. Her mother had given her directions, but Denise preferred to double-check with an online mapping service.

The residential area had nothing in common with her more humble, childhood beginnings.

"Wow!" Large houses, more like mansions, lined both sides of the road. Money was the tool between her and her parents. They used various amounts as her cause dictated. Her stepfather had his business, but had the family wealth. Her mother had class, but not a penny. Unlike her socialite sister, Denise worked in the city's government with its employee grades and job levels and notorious low pay. Her parents weren't impressed with her attempts to be independent. They thought it was better to take care of some things for their children.

A few more turns took her deeper into the neighborhood away from the main thoroughfare. Denise cruised at a pedestrian pace to read the house numbers. Finally, she braked in front of her new house. She looked in the rearview mirror, but saw no traffic. The street was eerily quiet, clean and orderly, as if it were ready for its place on a postcard. And this paradise was now home.

The driveway curved in a giant horseshoe, straightening in front of the spacious house, before disappearing through the foliage. The windows on the bottom level were oversize, and windows were in abundance on the second floor, where the roof peaked at sharp angles for a cathedral ceiling effect inside.

Denise saw that any further admiration had to be put on hold.

Scaffolding had been erected on one side of the house. Half of the roof tiles were stripped. The front door had been taken off the hinges and now sat on its side against the front of the house. The house was a wreck!

"Mom, it's me." Denise cradled the cell phone between her shoulder and ear. "I'm at the house. I don't see any other car so it looks like no one is here. The door…well, there's no door."

"Are you sure, dear? There should be an entire construction crew there."

"Yes. I'm in the car looking at it, but I can see that no one is here." Denise turned off the engine. "I'm going in to check. I'll call you back later."

"Be careful. Maybe you should let me stay on the phone, just in case."

Denise wasn't in the mood for her mother's statistical rundown of brutal crimes in Chicago and surrounding suburbs. Instead, she ended with a vague promise to call her back after investigating.

Her watch showed two o'clock. Lunch break was over. She pushed up her sleeves, ready for a fight with surly construction workers. Maybe she'd be lucky enough to sneak up on them throwing back a couple of beers.

Denise walked through the gaping doorway, then stood her ground with her hands on her hips as her gaze swept the foyer and living-room area. Signs of work were evident—additional scaffolds and partially constructed walls. Drop cloths covered various items.

She had to admit her parents knew what they were doing and were very good at it. They selected fixer-uppers, renovated them and then handed out a property to each child or resold it at a much higher value.

Closed double doors drew her attention. She opened them to admire a room framed with crown molding. From its position in the house next to the living room, she determined that it was the formal dining room.

"I don't cook, so I won't be using this room too much." Her voice echoed, magnifying the room's emptiness, a sad commentary on her life. She shrugged off her mind's attempt to wander down that path. *No, I will not go there—not today.*

Enjoying the sound of her shoes against the wood floors, she performed a short rendition of her sorority's popular step routine. Her hands clapped and smacked her thighs, accentuating the beats of her feet stomping against the hardwood floor in a rhythmic style that combined steps from hot musical groups with African traditional dances. The exertion left her panting and dying for a cold drink. She knew it looked crazy, but how could she resist the fun? There was just so much room here! Memories of her college days and Xi Theta Sigma flooded her mind. She shook it off and straightened her jacket. Growing up was a one-way, unyielding street, one she wasn't sure she was ready for.

Jaden Bond barely saw the lone figure enter the house. He'd heard a car pull up, but didn't get to the window fast enough. Despite craning his neck, he couldn't get a good line of sight. The unlit entryway provided enough shadow to disguise the person's identity. From his vantage point on the second floor, he moved a little closer to get a better view. The stranger crossed into a ray of light that cut through the large windows in a wedge shape across the floor.

His gaze narrowed. The telltale curves of the slim frame revealed part of the mystery. A woman, a stranger nonetheless, had entered the house.

She walked through the foyer and living room tapping the walls, brushing aside debris with her foot, then stood still with her hands stuffed in her jacket pockets studying the lower level.

Had the county sent an inspector? He wasn't in the mood for any bureaucratic crap. All the necessary permits had been obtained. Then again, she might be a nosy neighbor, a member of the home owners' association taking it upon herself to check on the property. Whoever she was, she'd now earned the label of trespasser.

When she disappeared into the formal dining room, he moved from his hiding spot. He didn't want to alert her that he was in the house—not yet. The way she moved around, her air of authority, intrigued him. What was she up to?

Suddenly, loud thumping sounds fractured the quietness. He slowed his approach, frowning with the effort to discern what made that rhythmic stomp. The dining-room doors remained partially opened. He eased them further open until he had a clear view of the woman, who was in full step mode. This unusual sight had him at a loss. Who walked into a house, selected a room and began stepping like the black Greek fraternities on campus?

He recognized some of the signature steps of Xi Theta Sigma sorority. On his campus, they were considered sisters to his fraternity. And he had to admit she was good. What if he started stepping? She'd probably freak. That would serve her right. When she paused to wipe her glistening forehead, he finally stepped forward with an irritable, authoritative demeanor for effect.

"Oh!" The woman jumped and stepped back until she hit the large, ornate mantel over the fireplace. Her gaze shifted from the door to him and back to the door. Her breathing sped up as she stiffened into a guarded stance.

"I'm Jaden Bond." He greeted her calmly, in even tones. "I'm renovating this house." Jaden waved his hand over the empty room. "What would you be doing here?" He pointedly looked down at her feet, which only seconds ago had been maneuvering in intricate steps with clean precision.

"I'm Denise." Her chin rose a smidgen. She stuffed her hands into her jacket pockets. "The hardwood floor looks good. I know that looked crazy...I was step mistress in university..." She chuckled, but it quickly died when he didn't respond. "I got carried away." Her hesitant tone had turned defiant.

Jaden didn't let the subtle change affect his decision. She was an annoying, albeit attractive, busybody who got caught nosing around someone else's property. "Your name?"

The woman tilted her head and in a flash turned a piercing gaze on him. Jaden accepted the challenge. Her attitude toward him was that *he* was the intruder. Maybe it was her snazzy suit and the way she crossed her arms as if staking her claim.

"Would you show me around the house?"

"Name?"

"Excuse me?" She tightened her crossed arms.

"I don't know you. I'd rather be personable when I show you the door."

"As if." The woman approached, moving across the room with a distinctive strut. "Look, I'm sure your boss mentioned my visit. I'll be living here."

Jaden frowned, unsure why this woman wanted to be mysterious. He knew his clients. They were old enough to be her parents. Maybe they were. He didn't trust easily, but he'd go along with her little game for a few more minutes, only out of curiosity. "Not a problem."

"Do you have a large crew working on this project?" She raised her eyebrows waiting for his explanation.

"Nah. It's pretty quiet at the moment."

"Given the amount of work left to be done, that may not be such a good thing."

"I've got it under control." Apparently, she was one of those types who figured she knew everything.

"We'll see if that's true." She walked past him with a small smile on her lips, as if she knew something that he didn't.

He quickly closed the gap as she exited the room. He hated to admit that this stranger intrigued him. She was pretty, but that wasn't it. The power suit probably meant corporate shark. The tight, neat ponytail shouted uptight personality. She was Type A, up close and personal. Maybe it was the slight sway of her hips as she moved in her stilettos that made him want to play along for a quick minute.

"Willing to give me the tour?" she asked over her shoulder.

"I've got the time." Jaden glanced down at his watch to verify his boast. His men would be returning to work the afternoon shift in thirty minutes. He'd wanted to finish writing up his status report before they came back. Playtime with this heiress apparent would have to end in ten minutes. He stepped up to walk beside her.

"The houses in this area were built in the boom days before the Depression wiped out families. The community catered to wealthy business owners. This neighborhood didn't have the homes for old money. You can imagine that the two groups of inherited wealth and the nouveau riche didn't mix."

"You know your local history."

Jaden shrugged. No need to boast about his neurosis of studying the historical background of his projects. He couldn't help adding, "The stock-market crash did a number on a lot of these families. Turned the social order of things on its head."

She turned to look at him. "Life has a way of bringing good out of evil." Her eyes, their fascinating blend of golden and light brown color framed by thick, dark lashes, held his.

"How philosophical of you," he teased.

"Life's observations, that's all."

Jaden could understand why the woman may not be impressed by the value of historical communities. Many people didn't appreciate the beauty of these Victorian and Edwardian homes, which had managed to survive both the initial suburban sprawl of bungalows, and now two-storied behemoths. Although this woman didn't look like she'd lived on the wrong side of the tracks, she didn't flaunt her membership in the upper income bracket. As a matter of fact, she seemed downright scornful.

"I suppose it's what the rich do with their money that is important," Jaden proposed.

"And when they manage to donate to charity, the motivating factor is mainly tax purposes."

"Not always. Er…Miss…I'm sure there are people with sincere philanthropic ideals." Jaden felt the need to counter, considering he had recently paid a significant sum to the Boys & Girls Club of America. Yes, it was tax-deductible, but the club had served as his haven when he was a teen.

His visitor snorted.

The attitude struck a nerve. "Haven't you ever donated something because it made you feel good?"

She shrugged and flipped her hair off her shoulder. "Tell me, what do you plan to do with this room?"

"Another personal question ignored," he muttered. Her evasiveness only made him wonder more about her. "The owner wants the room gutted and made into a media room." He added stress on the word *owner*, letting her know that he didn't consider her the owner.

"What? That's stupid."

For a couple of seconds, Jaden was speechless.

"You're quite full of opinions. You seem to be leaking a few, though. You might want to get that fixed."

"Sensitive. A handyman with a soft heart—who knew?" She rolled her eyes. "I think that maybe the room should be a library. You've certainly got the wall space to build large bookcases. Then have a large banker-style table in that corner." She pointed a slender, red-manicured finger at the desired area.

"An office is planned for the back of the house," he said. Her ten minutes were up.

"Now, that idea falls into the waste-of-space category."

"What difference does it make to you? Are you an interior designer?" He walked out of the room, expecting her to follow. He wanted to close the doors, literally and figuratively, on any further discussion. If she kept it up, he'd end his tour of the property, even if she did have a sexy way of pursing her lips before spouting her intrusive opinions.

"Maybe. Or maybe I'm a woman who knows what she wants."

Jaden led the way past the staircase toward the kitchen in the rear. "Well, that may be. But the owners also know what they want." The house copied the British style of closing off each major area into a private nook. Jaden paused in front of the double doors leading into the kitchen. He wanted the right amount of dramatic effect for his next revelation.

She folded her arms with a heavy sigh.

Jaden opened the doors, showing off the black-and-white tiled floor leading into the greater section of the kitchen. His father, always the practical observer, preached that the way to a woman's heart was in teasing her taste buds and creating a culinary addiction. The previous owner had invested in large commercial equipment with stainless-steel sleekness for this room.

His companion walked through the kitchen, opening and closing cabinets with an annoying, proprietary air. He wanted to pop that bubble. He cleared his throat, marking his displeasure. She hesitated only slightly before continuing with her inspection.

She actually pulled at a piece of wallpaper.

"Could you not do that?"

"It's ugly."

"But the owner didn't specify that the wallpaper needed to come down?"

He leaned in close to where she had torn the wallpaper. Now that would have to be repaired.

She turned to say something and then changed her mind. Instead she shook her head and walked toward the pantry. She opened the door and peered inside. Her head moved from side to side as she inspected the shelves. He thought about pushing her in and closing the door, but being arrested or losing the contract wasn't worth the satisfaction.

"The pantry is a good size, but the shelving could be redone," she suggested. "Change the spacing and you'll get more shelves in here."

"Who are you?"

"Denise Dixon, future resident of this house. I'll take over the details from my parents. You'll be meeting with me from now on, okay?" She extended her hand, wearing an easy grin like an annoying accessory. He briefly shook her hand, glad that she didn't have a limp grip, despite her other irritating features.

Jaden still couldn't respond without revealing his extreme irritation. As she closed the pantry door and breezed past him, the soft aroma of her perfume wafted up his nose. He didn't consider himself sophisticated enough to identify the scent, but he couldn't imagine ever forgetting that it belonged to her.

"Coming?" she prompted, heading out of the kitchen. "I'd like to see upstairs now."

Did he detect a hint of authority in her voice? "No." He shoved his hands into his pockets. "No, we need to correct a few things between us."

She turned to face him head-on. Her demeanor was unruffled, while his heightened irritation had him scratching his chin.

"The way I work with the Dixons, your parents, is that they give me a general idea of what they want. I add the right professional flair worthy of my expertise. I update them as I proceed. And at the end, they can inspect for final approval. You're coming into this agreement on the tail end. Any changes that you insist on will require a meeting of all parties." Jaden rocked back on his heels. "However, if you're expressing mere opinions, then I'll extend my appreciation for sharing your thoughts."

"Good. I'm glad to see your confidence. However, for clarity's sake, let me correct a misperception."

"Really." Jaden started to believe that this woman might as well be standing in front of a mirror repeating affirmations about power-tripping.

"I'm not offering opinions."

Jaden scratched his chin again. She was the right height for his gaze to glare down on her head.

"Let me reiterate that I'm Denise Dixon, daughter of the people who hired you, owners of the residence we're now standing in. Unlike my parents, I will not take whatever you throw out here. I know what I want. I will tell you what I want. Unless something is physically impossible, then I expect you to follow my wishes."

Quitting a project had never been an option for Jaden. It would mar his spotless reputation.

"Am I clear?"

"Yes, ma'am." Jaden squared his shoulders as he would have when facing a street fight during his teens. Most times he had emerged the victor. But Denise wasn't one of the guys, not with those sexy eyes and generous lips. *What a witch.* He imagined she'd fight dirty. And he wasn't sure he'd remain standing.

Denise didn't indulge her guilty conscience. Maybe she'd come off a bit like a black American princess. That wasn't her fault. Jaden Bond was to blame. He acted as if the house was his baby and no one could call it ugly.

She wasn't done with Jaden yet.

But for all her criticisms, she had to admit it: his work *was* impressive.

"What else would you like to see, Miss Dixon?"

"Denise will do."

"As you wish." He clicked his heels and bowed.

"You're not funny. I'm ready to see the upstairs." Denise didn't wait for permission. She climbed the stairs, fully expecting him to follow. When she didn't hear his accompanying steps, she paused. "What's the holdup?"

"Nothing."

Denise wondered what had brought on his small smile. She'd rarely seen a man blush, but his averted glance and tug at his collar gave her a hint. She'd caught him sizing up her rear view.

She'd remember to return the favor.

The second level of the house had been divided into small bedroom suites. Practical beige wallpaper and matching carpet covered the hallway.

"This is too ordinary." Denise walked down the hallway to the farthest room. "I want the style from downstairs to continue here." She opened the bedroom door and peered in, noting that it had its own bathroom.

"I'm glad you agree with my assessment." Jaden headed to the other end of the hallway. "You've got a lot of room with five bedrooms, each with an accompanying bathroom." His hand rested on a doorknob. "I'm sure that you'll have a lot to say about this room."

Denise stopped before entering, suddenly hesitant about entering the master bedroom—her room, her personal space—with this strange man in tow. Maybe if he weren't ruggedly handsome…

"I know the pasty pink is a turnoff. But you've got a massive amount of space, with the room situated over parts of the living room, dining room and kitchen." He walked around the room, directing her attention to the large beams in the ceiling, the huge fireplace and the window seats at each dormer window. Denise looked over at the area where she'd put her bed. Her king-size sleigh bed wouldn't overpower this room as it did in her apartment. Now she was starting to rethink that. Denise had only seen the house from the outside, but now that she was inside for the first time, she realized what her new lifestyle would be like. She'd be all alone in a huge bed, huge bedroom and huge house. She hoped the echo wouldn't be as pronounced when she moved in with her apartment furniture.

"The same wood as downstairs will be used for these floors. The colors will be vibrant. Similar molding as the first floor will also be in here. This room will rival any European boudoir. By the time I'm done in here, you won't want to leave this room."

Denise froze. "Excuse me?" Her voice came out
with a croak. Did she mistake the soft innuendo in
his bold statement? Or did his construction-worker
sex appeal do a number to her common sense?

Jaden tugged at his collar again. "I have a few
designs, that's all."

That's all, indeed. Denise took him all in. He
stood at about six feet, solid, and bold in all his
motions. *Damn, he was handsome.* She'd been so
busy looking at the house, she'd almost forgotten to
get a good look at him.

"When are you moving in? I was under the im-
pression that the house would be vacant for another
two weeks."

Denise shrugged. "The sooner, the better. I can
stay in one of the other rooms until this one's
complete." She'd already given notice to her apartment building. Her father, well, actually her stepfather, treated her financial episodes as causes for
lavish gifts.

"The previous owner must have a little British in
him." Jaden pushed open the bathroom door, looking
back at her expectantly.

Denise walked onto the crisp, white-tiled floor,
already liking what she saw. An oversize, deep
bathtub stood on a raised part of the floor like an
offering on Mount Olympus. No dings or bruises
marked the tub. "Oh, there's no showerhead."

Jaden ran his hand up the wall. "A showerhead can be installed here."

"Guess I'll be forced to enjoy long, soaking baths." Denise didn't need much coaxing to imagine the relaxing experience.

She stepped into the tub. She wanted to have a frame of reference for what this tub could do to soothe her nerves. She stooped in the tub, sitting on her haunches. The tub stopped at about shoulder height. All she needed was a good book, wine and a few candles for ambience.

"It's like a tank. Could be built for two." She suddenly imagined Jaden, a tall chocolate drop of mocha heaven, lounging in the tub with her.

"Well, I'll have to get back to my work." Jaden backed out of the bathroom, bumping his arm as he tugged at his shirt.

"What's the rush? I don't plan to strip and take a bath."

"And my men will be the better for it."

Denise followed Jaden out of the room. She took her time looking around, even checking out Jaden's body. The black jeans, worn in all the right places, the steel-toed construction boots that stirred her fancy for a rebel. She'd have to get her sorors up to the house to concur with her decision that her contractor could be any month's calendar pinup, preferably without the shirt.

As they walked downstairs, Denise said, "Thank you for indulging my requests. I'll wander around a bit." She offered her hand to Jaden with a big grin, signaling that she wasn't the total witch that he must have thought she was.

Jaden looked at his watch. "It was nice meeting you. Now that my men are back from lunch, I'm going to head downtown to meet with the landscaper."

"I'd like to go with you," she requested.

Then she flipped open her cell phone and dialed in to tell her work that she'd be out of the office for the remainder of the day. The truth was that she was having too much fun to return to the reality of her job—a city engineer dealing with the flooded streets, clogged storm drains and backed-up sewer pipes.

A glance at her watch had her place another call. She turned her back to Jaden and quietly spoke her instructions. She hadn't placed a bet in a while. What could a quick bet on a horse hurt?

"It is okay, right?" She felt compelled to ask since his shock, maybe dismay, with her request wasn't well hidden.

He looked at her, his gaze narrowing but steady. "Fine, as you wish."

"I wish," she added dryly. Obviously he didn't appreciate her company as much as she was starting to appreciate his.

Although Jaden had agreed to her company, his long strides through the house and out the front door said otherwise. Denise found herself almost tripping over her feet to keep up.

"What is the landscaper planning to do?" she asked for conversation's sake.

"Nothing fancy, as your parents suggested. A functional garden. Something low-maintenance that wouldn't cause you too much trouble with your busy, hectic lifestyle."

The answer bothered her. Too much about her was functional and operating within a rigid structure. Not until she saw this house, on a slight hill with its Old World elegance, had she tapped into a part of her that was whimsical and wanting.

They got in Jaden's car. When he turned the key, a country tune blared. "You don't strike me as a country-song type of guy." Denise bit back the urge to reach for the radio tuner and change to an R & B station.

"I usually crave what I can't get. I've always liked it, but Chicago isn't exactly the happening town for country music." He kept his eyes on the road, maneuvering deftly through the city's traffic.

"I can certainly understand that. I'm not a hater of country music. I used to sing the classics by Kenny Rogers, Glen Campbell, Tammy Wynette."

"Get outta here!" Jaden looked at her and snorted. "Can't believe that we're actually on the same page about one thing." He craned his neck to look up at the sky. "That might bring on the rain."

"And that reaction can get you hurt." Denise chuckled. Her body relaxed against the leather seat. "In my sorority I had to sing country songs for my Big Sister when I was a pledgee. Actually, it was to irritate her roommate. But she secretly liked Loretta Lynn. By the end of the six weeks, I'd learned quite a few songs and started collecting my favorites."

Jaden offered her a lopsided grin that added to the beauty of his profile, then broke out laughing.

"I can sing, you know." Denise agreed that the entire conversation had a humorous edge, but not worthy of Jaden's howl.

"I'm not doubting you." Jaden wiped his eyes. "You are a bundle of mixed messages. Big-haired country songs versus sleek corporate attire…"

"You had better be thinking of a compliment."

Jaden shrugged. "Maybe." He pulled out a roll of mints and offered her one.

Denise accepted the mint. "Do you like being the boss?"

"Somebody's got to do the job." A frown settled on Jaden's brow. "My business is my life. Although I don't expect my employees to share my vision or how to achieve that vision, I respect hard work. I don't like slackers. Can't stand them. People who take the shortcut through life had better stay out of my way." His lips tightened, as if he were putting an exclamation point on his statement of values. His hands gripped the steering wheel.

They arrived at the landscaping company, pulling into the crowded parking lot. Denise hopped out of the SUV as soon as Jaden turned off the engine.

"Sorry," Jaden said as they walked toward the landscaping company.

"For what?" Denise shrugged.

"The whole slacker comment. Didn't mean to sound judgmental. There's personal history."

Denise looked up at Jaden, more than a little curious.

"Stop looking at me like that." He playfully elbowed her. "Do you plan to accompany me on every phase of this renovation?" he asked, changing the subject.

"I might."

"It's not how I work." Jaden opened the office door for her.

Denise raised her chin and sashayed past him with a smirk.

"You must be quite a handful," he muttered as she passed.

To prove his indictment of her wrong, she remained fairly quiet during the meeting with the landscaper. Only when necessary did she interject, though not very often.

The plans Jaden and the landscaper created were flawless. The drawings of the house's exterior in the front and the back promised to accent its Old World elegance. The sophistication of the shrubbery design and carefully selected flowers stirred pride in Denise, for the first time, to be a homeowner.

"Anything you'd like to add?" Jaden turned to her with an expectant air. "I really stand behind what we've planned."

"I don't have a problem at all. It all sounds beautiful." Denise continued to observe as they discussed the top-three sample grass selections.

Any contribution in that area would make her sound foolish. Listening to their details, she'd hate to admit that she didn't know there were so many differences among the various grasses.

She stifled a yawn and stretched. Now bored with the direction of their talk, she walked around the office looking at numerous framed pictures of clients' properties.

Jaden's head was bent over a sample of turf. His passion for his work showed. His mannerisms reminded her of a professor. Yet his body and its movement and actions spoke of an athlete. His restrained discipline could be from a military back-

ground. Even his personal grooming had a fastidi-
ous neatness, like his hairline, trimmed to a sharp
edge around his face. No hint of afternoon shadow
along the jawline. His fingernails were neatly manicured.

"Denise." Jaden waved at her.

"Did you say something?" Her face warmed at
being caught openly staring at him.

"We're done here. Anything to add?"

"Nope. I'm cool."

They headed back to the house. Small talk marked
the ride, but she had difficulty concentrating. Her
hands worried the hem of her jacket as she wrestled
with following through on a whim. She was determined to add some spice, some impulsiveness, to
her life, especially her nonexistent love life.

"You're quiet."

"Just enjoying the ride. Thank you for taking me
along."

"Sure."

"What's your schedule for the remainder of the
week?" Denise attempted to navigate this unfamil-
iar terrain.

"I'll be there every day. I want to make sure that
we finish on time."

"By next week, right?" Whatever she planned to
do, it'd better be soon.

Jaden nodded, pulling into the driveway. The men had arrived and the property buzzed with activity. A man with design plans rolled and stowed under his arm waved at the car. Jaden responded with a wave, then looked at her. He appeared to want to say something, but instead his mouth tightened and his glance slid away from her.

"That's my project manager." He opened the car door and stepped out.

Denise experienced a momentary panic that a golden opportunity would be lost. She slid out of the car and hurried to the front where he waited for the foreman. "Look, Jaden," she said, "I'm not the type to be long-winded." She dug in her pocketbook and pulled out her business card. "How about going for drinks one evening? You can fill me in on other aspects of the plan." Her words tumbled out in order to beat the approaching foreman's arrival.

"A social thing?"

Now the foreman stopped between them. His eyes fastened onto the card that Jaden hadn't taken. Denise wanted to die.

"Bob, can you excuse us for one second?" Jaden finally took the card from her fingers. The foreman nodded and receded into the background.

"You are single, aren't you?" Denise asked, hoping the answer was negative. That would explain his reaction.

"Mixing business with pleasure is dangerous," Jaden responded, his voice low and deep, altogether serious.

"Figured by now you'd have realized that I'm not averse to risks. I'm a bit of an adventurer." She giggled to push aside the nervous jitters in her stomach. "Plus, the job is almost finished."

"You don't strike me as one of those women who propositions men. And, as far as the job goes, you never know what last-minute, time-consuming things may come up."

"'Those women.' That sounds terribly old-fashioned." Was he serious? She dared to look into his dark eyes. They didn't shift from her gaze.

Jaden tucked her card into his pocket. "I'm an old-fashioned guy."

"Come into the twenty-first century. I promise, it's not scary."

"I want to initiate contact, make the moves, take things to the next level."

"Following rules can be boring." She kicked at the dirt. "I promise, cross my heart, that I don't plan to ask you to marry me after a couple of martinis." His lack of enthusiasm stung and she wanted to sting right back.

"Okay, you got me there. I may have overreacted."

Jaden laughed. "Sure. I'll have a couple drinks. Now, could you let me get back to work? Or I may not finish on time."

"That might not be such a bad thing," she muttered, watching him walk away.

Chapter 2

In his office and lost in thought, Jaden's mind snapped back to his friend.

"I'm not talking for my health. If we're trying to get the community hospital account, we've got to stay on top of the city council and developers." Leonard Benson was the best electrician in the market. He had clients begging for his service. Their friendship had started before they became fraternity brothers and now they were as close as blood brothers.

"Are you going to the city council meeting tomorrow? Have you confirmed whether the hospital issue is on the agenda?" Jaden hoped that his friend had picked up the slack.

"I'll be there. I told you three days ago that the issue will be on the agenda. I also told you that the antidevelopment contingent will have a presence." Leonard, visibly a bundle of nerves, tapped a pen against his finger.

"See what feeding the deputy mayor can do?"

"And if I have to listen to one more of his boring stories, I'm going to quit and you'll have to deal with him." Leonard slapped Jaden's shoes off his desk.

"Staying late?" Jaden asked.

"No. The wife says I can't be late to another birthing class." Leonard started packing his briefcase. "You know traffic is going to be a bear if I don't get on the expressway before the hour."

"Go ahead. I'll shut everything off when I'm leaving. I may stay late to finish up some paperwork." He ran a tired hand through his hair. A huge yawn erupted. He slapped each side of his face.

"That's your problem." Leonard didn't pause in his cleanup. "This is the stage in your life when you should be settling down with a honey, maybe get married in a year or so and join me in the fatherhood club." Leonard paused in his task. "Keep it up and you'll wake up an old, lonely man, playing uncle to my child or, behind door number two, a two-for-one—high blood pressure and a heart attack."

"I think I hear Susan bellowing your name." Jaden cupped his hand to his ear.

"Susan doesn't bellow. At least I've got someone at home who takes care of me."

"Give me a break on the fairy-tale stuff. You're about to see a different side to Susan that's been reserved for after you have kids."

"You're talking from a world of experience, right?" Leonard snorted and waved off Jaden's remarks. "Why is it hard for you to settle down? You barely have dates, insisting on calling them business meetings. Don't you feel the need for some loving from a good woman?"

"Do those come in one-day servings?"

"Don't knock it. You've been stuck in this funky phase of life for too long."

Even though Leonard pointed his finger at him, and looked as if he wanted to knock him on his butt, Jaden refused to budge from his stance. He didn't have to make sense, especially to his frat brother.

Leonard grabbed a handful of various documents from Jaden's desk. "It's always work. You can't bury yourself behind paperwork. You're not the type to obsess about wealth. So what is it?"

"Nothing!"

Leonard raised his hand in surrender. As usual, his face was easy to read. The shock still registered—his eyebrows shot up in raised arches.

"Oh wise one, save it for the big O. Maybe she'll invite you to her TV couch and you can unload your feel-good philosophy," Jaden taunted.

"Some days you can be a horse's backside. I'm going to be late."

Leonard's stage of life didn't match Jaden's. They now belonged on different spectrums. How could Leonard possibly understand the burden of Jaden's responsibility? Aging parents brought along certain sacrifices. Being the sole breadwinner because of his brother's messed-up life demanded that he stay focused. Whenever he had to, he rid himself of distractions, including those of the female persuasion.

His friend had no clue how far his brother had sunk. Jaden was too ashamed to share the full details. He squeezed his eyes shut to shake off his feelings. "Have fun birthin'," he said with forced lightness.

After Leonard left, the mood in his office floated down, like a balloon losing buoyancy. His friend's hard message coupled with his fatigue turned Jaden's mood sour.

Since he still had more projects to investigate and determine if he wanted to bid on them, he had to find a way to beat back the blues. He turned on the music downloaded on his computer and raised the volume until the bass pounded to blast away the quietness. After listening to hip-hop—a little Roots and Talib Kweli—he went with what his soul craved, the blues. For a few minutes, he got comfortable in the chair and then succumbed to the haunting B. B. King lyrics and their underlying languid melodies.

Listening to the blues took him back to his childhood, when life was rough and unpredictable. While his parents were always loving to their family, they'd struggled to make ends meet pretty much all of his life. Some weeks or months, his parents' unemployment overlapped. Jaden's good grades set their minds at ease about him. And his dad loved listening to the blues.

Now his business successes allowed his parents to live in reasonable comfort with frequent vacations. That sense of hopelessness he'd witnessed, of having to live paycheck to paycheck, that cloying fear of losing a home, gave him the strength and focus for his work ethic.

Too bad his brother didn't share the same diligence.

An hour later, he reached a manageable point with his tasks. Now he'd head home and crash for a few hours before starting his day all over again. He thought about what Leonard had said and about meeting feisty, pretty Denise days earlier.

Leonard's accusations still bothered him.

Before he could second-guess his actions, he reached for the phone and dialed. After the phone started ringing, he realized how late it was, a good reason to hang up.

"Hi, Jaden." Denise answered on the third ring.

"Oh."

"Your name popped up on the caller ID," she explained.

"I didn't mean to interrupt you." In person, her husky voice went with her no-nonsense image. Over the phone, the huskiness had a unique earthy quality, bordering on sensual. *How erotic.*

"Hey, don't go silent on me."

"Sorry, it's late. My brain isn't working too hot." His words were tied up in knots. He gritted his teeth and stayed the course. "I'm calling to see if you're free for dinner, instead of drinks."

"What about right now? I kind of expected you to call me two days ago."

Jaden laughed. Denise was a blast to his system. "You know of any late-night restaurants?"

"Yep. Feel like Jamaican?"

His stomach rumbled after she gave him the name and address. His pastrami sandwich at lunch was long gone. "I already know what I want: jerk chicken, peas and rice, and nice cold beer. See you in thirty minutes?"

"See you then, and don't think you don't owe me drinks."

Jaden hung up and pumped his fist. A little victory celebration in the end zone had to be done.

Leonard would be proud.

As he filed his paperwork and cleaned off his desk, he hummed a Muddy Waters tune. The singer crooned about a dangerous girl who had witching power to scramble his brains and suck his will with her devilish ways.

But he hadn't gone that far. Not too many women had managed to make him think seriously about any type of long-term relationship. Truthfully, that applied to short-term relationships, too. He had perfected the art of keeping things casual.

Denise slapped a high five with Naomi after snapping shut her phone. "And to think that we were actually trying to find a reason to call him." She did a quick two-step in celebration, bopping to her own happy beat. "Okay, now I've got to figure out what to wear."

"That depends on a lot of stuff." Naomi walked over to the closet that was the entire second room in the apartment. "When did you get this black dress? I like!" Naomi held a delicate, flimsy slip of material.

"I know that look. You're not borrowing anything

else from me. I'm still waiting for my capri pants from last summer."

"I didn't think you wanted them back."

"Don't even try that with me. I'm coming over to your place unexpectedly and I'm going to retrieve my clothes."

"They probably won't fit, anyway." Naomi made a face. "Looks like there might be extra junk in the trunk."

"You're a sorry excuse for a soror." Nevertheless, Denise slid her hand over her rump and groaned.

"I know. I'm bad. Forgive me." Naomi pouted. Her full remorse was suspect, given the mischievous twinkle in her eyes. She stretched across the daybed, propping her head up with one of the pillows. "I'll leave, if you want."

"Yeah, sure looks like you're going somewhere." Denise chose lowrider black pants, a black tank top, a lightweight pashmina shawl and sparkly high-heel sandals. Black made her feel sexy. Plus, in black, her butt wouldn't look as if it needed its own trailer. "Grab the phone if it rings while I step into the shower."

"Sure." Naomi's attention was already diverted to a TV show featuring biographies of the latest top-ten Hollywood hunks.

Denise merely shook her head at the nonsense. She never cared for the polished and glitzy packaging of any guy. A man who cared about the smoothness of his skin, the perfect arch in his brow, or fretted about his next facial appointment didn't gel with her wish list. Nothing about Jaden belonged with the metrosexual label.

He scored high on all the right qualities. On a physical level, he had the power to turn up her senses a notch. Intellectually, he was a thinker. He cared about the world and his contribution to it. She'd dated enough self-indulgent morons. He was a refreshing breath to her system.

Anything else about him, she looked forward to discovering. Like whether he was a hot kisser. Whether he held a woman by her shoulders or scooped her into a passionate embrace. Was he the type to close his eyes? Did he suffocate with his tongue? Or did he stroke like an expert lover? Could he make her insides quiver and the tips of her breasts tighten with anticipation?

She turned on the shower and stepped in, turning up the cold water for the crisp, shocking blast. Her thoughts had moved from imagining Jaden kissing her to him sliding his hands down the length of her body, cupping her behind as they shared a searingly hot, passionate kiss.

She tilted her head back, allowing the water to beat against her neck. Under the spell of her thoughts about Jaden, she spread the body-wash lotion along her shoulders, over her breasts, cupping them under the onslaught of the water.

She smeared more sudsy lotion down her stomach and slid her hand between her legs, washing and stroking. Stroking and washing. The sensitive lips quivered and swelled under her ministrations. She slid in her fingers, bathing her inner self in the process.

With her eyes closed, she pictured him pleasuring her. It wouldn't be her fingers, but instead his, within her—reaching to the sensitive spot that had its own desire to be touched and prodded.

She rested her foot on the tub's edge and increased the friction, wondering what it would feel like to have Jaden's tongue intimately explore her until she exploded, like she was doing now.

Not a bad fantasy.

Once she had achieved a semblance of control, she stepped out the shower. She only had a few minutes to dress and apply her makeup without being late.

Naomi peeped around the corner of the bathroom door. "Use the charcoal pencil. It'll give you a sultry look."

Denise offered a small, appreciative smile. "Could you do my hair?"

"Would love to."

Denise handed her the hair lotion that softened her

hair and allowed for it to be worn pulled back and up. "I'll wear the silver accessories."

"Are you trying to conquer him?"

"I sound desperate, don't I?" Denise groaned. She pulled a tissue out of the box. "I'm too made-up. Too dressed up. I look like a joke," she wailed.

"You sound hormonal. I want to meet this man who has you acting…girly." Naomi pulled the tissue out of her hand. "Don't mess up my good work." She kissed her lightly on her cheek. "Go do your thing."

They admired the full effect of their grooming. Denise smiled, happy with the overall look.

"I'll make you proud, soror." Denise gathered her keys. "You're welcome to crash here."

"As much as I'd like to stay here and hang out, I've got to get up early for practice tomorrow. Then we head to Michigan to play."

They walked down to the garage, exchanging small talk about the other sorority sisters. They'd made promises to keep in touch and stay close after college. But every year since graduation, they seemed to be drifting apart, going down separate paths and not able to spend much time together.

"Promise me that you'll call me with the details. I don't want to have to wait until I'm back in town." Naomi hugged her.

"Here he comes," Denise announced Jaden's arrival for her own benefit. Her nervous system needed a warning.

"Introduce me," Naomi insisted. Denise knew she didn't have a choice. She supplied the introductions as quickly as possible. Thank goodness Naomi didn't try to be funny and stick around to ask embarrassing questions. In fact, she left pretty quickly.

"You look stunning."

Denise blushed. "Thank you." For heaven's sake, she sounded like a Hollywood bimbo with her breathless response. She cleared her throat. "Punctual. I like that."

"I called ahead for reservations."

"Not necessary." Denise couldn't recall any time that she was unable to get seated at Jamaican Joe.

"Didn't want to take the chance and not be able to eat because it's crowded. I don't like surprises. And I am hungry." Jaden maneuvered through the night traffic, which got thicker as they headed closer to the city.

"I bet you plan your entire week in advance," she teased.

"I'm not answering that." Smiling, he turned to face her as a red traffic light halted further progress. "Were you heading out before I called?"

"No, why?"

The traffic light switched to green.

"Just wondering." He didn't say anything more until he parked and came around to her side of the door. She took his outstretched hand.

"You're staring."

"Hmm." He didn't apologize. However, when her hand went self-consciously to her hair, he gently pulled it away. "You look fantastic."

"Sir, may I park your car?" A valet interrupted any further dribbling compliments he was on the verge of making. Jaden tossed him the key, took the ticket and followed Denise into the restaurant.

The ambience clearly wouldn't usher in a romantic interlude. Bright fluorescent lights, lots of late-night eaters and a boisterous staff created a din. Yet, the reggae music and tropical-island theme resonated, and the glorious smell of tasty food made the restaurant the right pick.

The host led the way, weaving a path between tables to a booth. The curved seats faced out so diners could view and be viewed by the patrons. Jaden didn't know whether to slide into the middle or remain on the edge. This night out shouldn't be any different from his other dates. But with Denise, he wanted to be careful and follow his internal guidelines. *Casual, man, casual.*

"I'm really glad we came here," Denise said.

"Me, too. The setting reminds me that I haven't taken a vacation in a long time."

"Have you ever been to Jamaica?"

"Key West is about as far as I got." Her attitude spoke of a world traveler. He didn't need to ask, but did anyway. "What about you?"

She waved her hand. "I've been around."

"Like where? I think the places that a person chooses to hang out or work in reveal a lot about that person."

"Whoa, that's heavy. I'm not sure I should tell."

The waitress stopped and took their drink orders. Jaden chose a soda, and when she ordered a glass of wine, he could already feel her questioning his choice. "I'm waiting," he reminded her.

"I did a student exchange to France. I've been to Ghana with a book club. Then, I've been to several Caribbean islands with my sorors and as part of a cruise."

"Any other place that you want to go?"

"Egypt. I want to see all the historical sites and the pyramids." She accepted her wine from the waitress and took a sip. "Don't you want to see new places beyond the United States?"

"Sure. But I have to work."

"And I don't?" Denise frowned.

"That's not what I meant. I wasn't finished. 'I have

to work' is not just a statement about my work ethic. I also support my parents and never felt comfortable about leaving them. They're getting pretty elderly."

"Oh, wow. Sorry. I sounded like a shrew. That's amazing that you take care of them like that."

Jaden shook his head. "Let's order."

They placed their order, opting for the special of the day—tilapia baked in garlic and butter, served with peas and rice and fried plantains.

Their conversation died. They both watched the other patrons, heavily engaged in conversation with much laughter. Jaden didn't know why he felt so uptight and nervous, but he struggled to think of something to say. A nearby couple who shared a passionate kiss over their half-eaten meal had him tugging at his collar. He shifted his gaze back to Denise, who openly studied him.

"What do you want to know?" Jaden asked.

"Wondering why a good-looking man, successful business owner, doesn't have a line of women scrambling over each other to attach herself to him. I have girlfriends who would pay to be with a man like you."

"Why don't you think that has happened?"

Denise set down her glass and leaned forward. "I don't think you're that type. Conservative. Play by the books. See things black or white."

Her eyes looked so darn sexy with their shimmery

shading. He enjoyed every feature of her face, from her smoky eyes to her sharply defined mouth and glossy lips.

"Thanks for making me sound boring." Jaden chuckled.

The food arrived on large platters. The waiters set each plate down with a flourish. Steam rose along with the heady scent of herbs and spices. The fish looked tender and tasty.

"What's the matter?" Denise set down her fork.

"I should have gotten the salad. I haven't eaten a salad today." He looked imploringly at the waitress.

She nodded and left.

"You just proved my point. You *do* plan everything!" Denise sat back with her arms folded.

"I'm not trying to have stomach issues late tonight, while you're snoring away."

"I promise I don't snore," Denise taunted.

"And how would you know?"

"Well, you could stick around to see if I'm true to my word." Denise accepted her refilled glass of water from the waitress, picked up her fork and began to eat. She never took her eyes off Jaden. She enjoyed flirting with him to see the flashes of shock and embarrassment that he worked hard to conceal.

"May I ask why you are still single? Seems like you would have no problem selecting your mate."

"You make me sound like a shark." Denise leaned back to give herself a break from the constant shoveling of food into her mouth. The food was too delicious to linger.

"Far from a shark. I don't think that you are cold-blooded." Jaden poured dressing on the salad he had just gotten. He raised his fork to his lips, then paused. "You're determined."

"And you're not used to a woman showing determination?"

Jaden shrugged, choosing that moment to fill his mouth.

Denise joined him, willing to get through this conversation at his pace. Jaden was a challenge. And she was up for it.

"The sweet potato soufflé smells good."

"Want to try a little?" Denise pushed her plate toward him.

"Maybe just a little."

"Go ahead," she encouraged him. As if to help him along, she ate another forkful. "It's really good. Almost like my mother's and I wouldn't tell her that."

"Your mother is from the islands?"

"Both parents are from Jamaica, but came to the U.S. when I was in second grade."

"Your accent is gone."

"Depends on whether I'm talking to my family."

She wiped her fingers on her napkin. "Or when I'm in an emotional state," she said with a grin. "Yo know wat a talkin' 'bout, mon."

"Cool. Do you think that you'll ever go back to live?"

"I doubt it. I'll visit because there is still family. But I'm building my career here. Yet you never know where you may end up."

"What's your career?"

"Engineer. I work for the city in their public works division."

"Wow, I would have never picked engineer."

Denise hated to think what career he'd pick for her.

"Hey, I didn't mean anything bad. You just seemed as if you'd be in the corporate world. Vice president or even president."

"In other words, bossing people around." She picked up her fork to threaten him.

"You're stretching the intent of my words." He held up his hands in surrender, but didn't hold back on the wide grin. Relaxed, he didn't have the imposing air. Now he seemed boyishly handsome. *Maybe not boyishly,* she thought, as she focused on his full lips twitching with laughter.

"Let's go to a safer subject. Tell me about your parents," Denise requested.

"Not much to tell. They're retired now. Still living

in the same house from my childhood. Sometimes I get lucky and get them out to go take a vacation. Myrtle Beach is their favorite spot."

"Good to see parents happily married and enjoying life together after all this time." Her parents were together, but enjoying each other would be stretching things. "How about siblings? I have two." His reaction caused Denise to cut short her explanation about her sister and brother. She didn't miss the subtle tightening of his mouth. His gaze drifted away from the table. A carefully composed expression did little to fool her that this personal subject did not bother him.

He finally responded, "I have a younger brother."

Denise nodded. "I'm sure they're proud of your success. Business owner. Eligible bachelor. Parents always want what's best."

"Yeah, my mother would rather that I wasn't a bachelor. I'm messing up her timeline of being a mother-in-law and grandmother, in that order, she's quick to stress." If Denise wasn't mistaken, Jaden was a mama's boy. Whenever he mentioned her, he grew gentle.

"Are your parents proud of you?" Jaden suddenly turned the attention back on her.

Denise shrugged. "I'd like to think so." Her lie was necessary. Otherwise, what would he think about how she'd come close to disgracing the family, and how they struggled with their disappointment in her.

"I feel that my parents worked hard to give me what they could," Jaden said. "Now it's my turn to have them reap the benefits."

"Why are you so perfect? Are you heading for the seminary?" Denise set down her fork, her appetite satiated. She'd have to get the remainder of the food to go, otherwise she'd burst.

"Far from perfect, I'm afraid," Jaden said. "But I'm more cautious than most."

"And I think that life is too short for double meanings and unsaid words."

Jaden didn't respond. Instead, he waved his hand at the waitress who appeared with their bill.

"How much?" Denise opened her pocketbook.

"I'll pick up the tab, of course."

"Thank you. I expect that we'll be heading for those drinks on Thursday. We can talk more about house plans." Denise threw it out there. She didn't want to dwell on whether he would call or if she should call. His answering nod set her mind at ease.

They left the restaurant. Denise was surprised that they'd stayed barely over an hour. Now the evening would end and Denise wasn't ready to say goodbye.

She looked over at Jaden as he drove her back to her house. He didn't say much. His mood had grown quiet. She tried small talk, but couldn't seem to draw him out of his contemplative mood.

When he pulled in front of her apartment, they sat quietly.

Maybe he wasn't interested, she thought. She'd had to beat away most men she'd dated, and had to be rude to get them to back off. Jaden remained too calm, setting off her alarm. Instead of intriguing him, she probably irritated him.

Now they were parked. Denise waited with her hand on the door handle. The problem was that she didn't know how long she should wait or exactly what she was waiting for.

Jaden kept the engine running, not wanting to give her the wrong idea that they'd start necking in the car. She was a classy woman and shouldn't think that he was coarse and freaky. Yet, he desperately wanted to kiss her. The color she had on her lips incited an imagining vision—his lips covering hers.

"Well, I'll be going." Denise opened the door and slid out.

Jaden opened his mouth to call out to her. He got out of the car and followed her into her building. "The bathrooms have all been updated at the new house. Most of the first floor is done. We might even finish early, by a couple of days."

Denise didn't respond.

He frowned, noting that her pace quickened. Talking about the house fell flat. "I'm looking forward to hanging out on Thursday."

"Why?"

"Why! I thought we had fun tonight. I enjoyed your company. I love the way you enjoy your food."

"You mean stuff my face." She smiled, put her key in her lock and offered him her hand. "Thanks for inviting me."

Jaden looked down at her hand. He realized that his reservation was over-the-top. Not all women had ulterior motives. Denise was far from being a ditzy, gold digger. Her family had impressed him or he wouldn't have taken the job. And she more than impressed him with her style, drive and quest to live her life uninhibited.

He took her hand and kissed the top. For now, that's what he could manage without grabbing her arms and pulling her into his embrace. "Good night, Denise." He touched her chin and let his hand fall to his side. "Sweet dreams," he whispered.

Sweet dreams! That wasn't such a tall order to fill. She leaned against the closed door, not daring to look through the keyhole to watch Jaden depart.

She had practically melted at the knees, half hoping that he'd lean over to kiss her lips because she looked that darn good. With all his talk about how he lived his life straight down the middle, she had resisted pulling him into her apartment with a lip-lock out of this world.

When she could move away from the door, she headed for the window to see him leave. After several minutes, the car still hadn't appeared. She couldn't have missed his departure. Maybe he was having problems getting his car started.

She'd better check on him. Grabbing her keys, she opened the door and walked into a solid wall of muscle. Her muffled cry meshed with a deep grunt.

Strong hands grasped her shoulders, providing a steadying support. The scent of familiar cologne revealed the unexpected visitor's identity.

"Jaden, what are you doing here?" She looked up into the dark brown eyes that shimmered with a sexy glint. Their power sucked her body into a limp mass and made her step closer. Her hands were already plastered against his chest. Her fingers clawed at his shirt, one step ahead of her brain.

For the life of her, she had to concentrate on his words. All she saw were his full lips and flashes of his teeth.

"I want to kiss you."

"I want you, too." She forgot to say "kiss," but she wanted that, too.

Denise tilted her head to anticipate Jaden's mouth, which kissed her softly on the corners of her lips. He lingered on those spots, while she squeezed her eyes shut to keep from moaning.

Her hands slid under his arms, reaching around his body. His muscles tensed and relaxed as her fingers roamed the width of his back. Her body responded with equal sensitivity as his hands rested on her waist and slowly slid down her hips.

He took his time. She adored the languishing strokes of his lips, warm and attentive, moving with enough pressure to ignite desire from her body's core.

Impatient for more than foreplay, she opened her mouth, casting an unspoken invitation. His tongue accepted. Her mouth was teased with a light flurry of strokes. The small ignition of desire crackled with the life of a wildfire, sending out signals to the tips of her breasts, crushed against his chest, to the tingling flutter in her stomach, fit snugly against his body.

His hands held her hips in place. The need for this man, beyond a heated kiss, more than his hands learning the curves of her body, washed over her with the strength of a tidal wave. With a groan that started deep in her throat, she plunged her tongue in his mouth. Now wasn't the time to think about the rigid dance of dating rules.

Denise almost fell when Jaden broke contact. The heat that they generated between them dipped. Coolness from the air-conditioned surroundings helped drag her back to reality. Hard, unsympathetic reality flooded in, replacing the warm, sensual vibes.

"I only wanted to say that I really enjoyed the evening," Jaden offered. His voice sounded deeper and husky.

Denise accepted that she couldn't jump his bones when this wasn't even the first official date. She'd never been with a man so soon after she'd met him. Yet Jaden wasn't the average male specimen.

"Me, too," she murmured.

Sleep didn't come easy. All her senses tingled on edge. She paced, but her mind raced as she tried to understand what she was feeling. How could this man scramble her thoughts, spike her heartbeat, turn her thoughts into incoherent ramblings.

She flicked on the computer, logging on to the Internet. She didn't stop pacing until the familiar page popped onto the screen. For another hour, she gambled. Lost some money, won a little, until a couple thousand had been sucked out of her account.

The guilt that grew exponentially after each act demoralized her. She couldn't sleep, disgusted with what she'd done. Her nerves craved calm order, but her conscience ate away, leaving her cranky. Finally she couldn't stand it anymore and drove to her soror's house. Only when she was on her way did she call Sara. She'd done crazier things than driving thirty minutes into the boonies to see Sara.

On the quiet back roads, the memory of a heated kiss kept her alert and more than a little warm. Her face blushed as she deliberated over her body's responses.

Sara answered the door in her dressing gown, a not-so-subtle hint that Denise ignored. "I've had quite a night, let me tell you." She followed Sara into the apartment, heading for the kitchen. "You have any herbal tea? That raspberry fru-fru stuff would be perfect."

Sara good-naturedly pushed her out of the way. She moved through the kitchen, preparing tea for both of them. Denise opened the pantry door and stared at the various items on the shelves until she found her target—shortbread Chessman cookies.

"Okay, let's go chat about me." Denise pinned the bag of cookies under her arm and followed Sara with the teacup and hot water to the living room.

"You're obviously excited. This had better be good."

"Better than good," Denise exclaimed, nibbling on a cookie.

Sara's eyes narrowed into slits. Her smile disappeared. "You'd better not tell me that you need money."

Sara's blunt remark cut deep into Denise's euphoric state.

"That was rude of me." Sara reached over and patted Denise's knee. "I'm afraid I sound like the person who always reminds you of past ills."

Denise set down her teacup and waited for the shame to subside. Considering her behavior in the past and secretly in the present, she couldn't blame Sara's statement.

"I promise not to be a pain in your butt. I'm all ears." Sara gave her an apologetic grin. "What has you glowing?"

Sara snuggled deeper into the couch. She reached for the box of cookies. "I'm listening."

"Okay. Met this guy. He's cool, kind of laid-back."

"Where'd you meet?"

Denise bit her lip, knowing what would come after disclosure. "He's hired to renovate the house."

"The new house? The one that your parents bought for you. Aren't you crossing the line? This is priceless." Sara's laugh poked at Denise's own insecurities about what she was doing.

"He is not the hired help. He owns the company. Grow up, Sara!"

"Wonderful, you can rack up leadership skills on your accomplishments list, along with other sexy tidbits. Wicked."

"You're sounding like a teenager." Denise tried to remain stone-faced, but her friend was right. Her giddiness practically bubbled over. Her conversation would fare better if she didn't erupt into a fit of giggles.

"I suspect that you wouldn't come over late at night to talk about something that was perfect." Sara sipped her tea, keeping a keen eye on her. "What's the problem?"

"I was practically ready to jump his bones. And you know that's not my style. Don't get me wrong, I speak my mind and don't like to play games, but I'm also not a nympho." She looked up to gauge Sara's reaction. Sensing that she sincerely was listening, Denise continued. "We're both mutually attracted to each other. But he's slow to make the first move, although tonight's finale hinted at the potential of some pretty hot moves."

"Details, please. Hugged? Kissed? Jumped into bed?" Sara counted on her fingers.

"You're taking all the fun out this and making it sound cheap. We kissed, Miss Nosy. But it was more than a kiss and those details, I'm keeping to myself."

"Okay, be that way. So far everything is pointing in the positive direction." Sara refreshed their teacups with hot water.

Denise selected a fresh tea bag.

"Stop thinking so hard. You admitted that this guy

makes you happy. Don't try to second-guess him. Relax and let things happen on their own."

Unlike Sara's happy ending with her college sweetheart, Denise had a harder outlook. Her experiences had carved a strong stance toward commitment. A strong friendship was all she could offer, anything deeper was an impossibility.

People lived without committing to each other. And they managed.

Denise settled more comfortably into the chair. "Enough about me. What's going on in your crazy world? How's life with Jackson?"

"I'm doing fine. Wish that he was here more often. He'd promised me that he'd move up here. I'm trying not to read anything into the fact that he's not here."

"I'm sure that you've nothing to worry about. Keep communication open. You didn't come all this way in your relationship to backslide. You're the perfect couple. And may I add that you're the only one out of our line sisters who can actually say they have a boyfriend. We didn't do all that work to get you college sweethearts back together, for you to have a breakup. Plus, I want to be a bridesmaid in a fabulous gown." Denise made a big performance of running her hands over hips and pushing up her chest.

Sara nodded, the lack of confidence evident in the slight droop of her shoulders.

Chapter 3

Jaden stared at the cell phone, a bit amazed at himself for calling Denise and admitting that she occupied his thoughts. He was always cautious about starting any kind of relationship.

His financial status attracted the wrong women. Some women he was sure shared genes with a bloodhound. They practically sniffed the air before zeroing in on him. The bright gleam in their eyes had nothing to do with him. It had to do with dollar signs.

Through many trials and even more errors, gradually he distanced himself from babe magnets like bars, nightclubs and fitness gyms. His friends thought him crazy to miss out on the high ratio of females in the city. They made the dating scene sound like an all-you-can-eat buffet.

He wished that he'd already undergone this life-style change before falling for Charlene, the leech who'd attached herself and squeezed him dry. It hadn't taken him long to know that they were on a road that could only end badly for him. She'd tried everything and, for the most part, it had worked to keep him at her side. Even now, he reaffirmed that he had never been in love with her. She knew this, too. But for her purposes, love didn't matter. She'd had her life planned and he was the involuntary charac-ter in her play of a perfect family—father, mother and her child, a son. He often wondered how Demetrius was doing. His desire to see the boy warred with the actions that his visit would elicit from his mother.

Denise had him breaking all his rules. He enjoyed a strange mix of heady anticipation and tingling fear of the unknown.

He liked Denise. Her looks, her drive and how easy she was to talk to at dinner. He refused to allow his personal drama to suffocate his attempt to con-nect with her. Now, a few nights later, he'd invited her to his house for a home-cooked meal.

"This place should be in a magazine," Denise blurted when she entered. She was amazed with the decor, order and neatness of the place—no dust bunnies in sight.

"It's been featured in several national and local ones. Now I politely refuse. I don't like feeling like a walking advertisement for women to approach."

"Now, that sounds …"

"Rude?"

"No. Blunt." She looked around the room, estimating the cost of the furniture, window dressing, decorations, wall paintings. This place, along with Jaden, would be considered a mother's dream for her daughter. "Why do I get a personal tour? I may be after your deep pockets."

"Maybe I'm the one looking at your deep pockets," he replied.

"Touché, but that is my parents' money. I'm a humble government worker."

"Have a seat." Jaden crossed the room to pick up a remote. With the push of a button, he'd turned on the CD player. "Mood lights?" He didn't wait for her response before pressing a button, and the lights automatically dimmed to a soothing glow.

"Will any of those buttons produce a glass of white wine?" Denise glanced around the room, waiting for some secret hiding place to be revealed with a minibar.

"Sure. I do have a small collection in the basement. One sec." Jaden disappeared through a door, his footsteps fading as he descended to what must have been a wine cellar.

"He can't be this darn perfect." She quickly walked around the living room and into the open-design dining room and kitchen. In any one of those areas, the guests could see each other. Given the apparent size of the house from the outside, she wondered what the remaining rooms featured.

Jaden reappeared with two wineglasses and a bottle of wine. "One of my favorites. It's a wine from a small vineyard in Texas, outside of Houston, if you can believe it. But very tasty."

Denise waited until he'd poured the wine. "Here's to trying new things."

"No risk. No reward," Jaden added.

They clinked glasses and then took a sip for their toast. Denise was surprised by the mellow taste of the wine, expecting it to be dry. Instead, sweet. He had selected a good choice for the occasion. She took another appreciative sip.

Denise took a seat, opting for a high-backed single chair. She snuggled against it, enjoying the wine that slowly relaxed the tension. She was glad that Jaden stopped his nervous pacing to sit opposite her.

"What do you want to know about me?" Denise asked, purposely keeping her tone gentle.

Jaden swirled the wine in his glass. "That you may wind up wanting more from me than I can offer."

"I used to want the world and then some." Denise drained her glass and set it down. The wine warmed her. "Now, I live with only the present in mind." She didn't expect to have deep, philosophical conversation at this time of night.

"Has a man broken your heart?" Jaden asked.

"My heart has been broken." Denise nodded. "But I wouldn't call him a man. What about you? How many hearts have you broken?"

"I'm not sure that organ existed or even worked in some of the women I dated."

"We're quite a battle-weary couple." She held up her glass for seconds.

"I've got something perfect for our recovery." Jaden walked over to the bookcase along the wall. "Do you like poetry?"

Denise gave a lukewarm nod. "Are you sure that you're not a professor?"

"Why would you say that?" Jaden was engrossed with his search. His hand dragged along the spines of books. He paused, then shook his head and continued until he got to the end of the row.

"Can't remember ever reading poetry for the sheer pleasure." Denise hoped that he wouldn't launch into a lengthy analysis of poets. She knew only a handful of poets and less about poems. Now, if he wanted to talk about movies, she'd jump all over it.

"After a long day, I relax with a glass of wine and a book of poetry. It clears my head. Refills my tank when I feel emotionally spent over things I can't control." He selected a book, flipped through the pages and stopped at a page that interested him. "I really like this one." He retook his seat and read the poem aloud.

Denise didn't care for abstract verses like the one he was reading. However, the smooth, velvety tones of Jaden's voice and striking rhythm of the verse had the same effect as the alcohol in her system. When he was done, she waved for him to continue. "I need peeled grapes to make this complete," she teased. "Did some past lover turn you onto poetry?" Denise pushed the question through the fuzziness of her mind. She was so relaxed and contented to listen to Jaden.

"You're persistent and way off course."

And just like that, Denise wanted to kiss Jaden. Being with him was like doing a belly flop, undignified and forceful into the deep end of the pool. If she looked up through the watery surface, reality would be there waiting for her. Instead, she'd rather enjoy learning about this intriguing man who had the rare qualities of being drop-dead gorgeous with a working brain.

"My mother turned me onto poetry."

The statement seemed innocent enough. However, Jaden didn't elaborate any further.

"Read some more." She surprised herself with the request. But with soft music in the background, a liberal supply of wine and satisfying company, she could get into this poetry vibe. Not that she dismissed the bonus of having Jaden's one-on-one attention.

For the next ten minutes, Jaden moved on to another book and read poetry that revealed someone's yearning for love that would never be returned. At the end, Denise set down her glass.

"Look, you're going to have to find a poem that doesn't leave me feeling like I need to bawl in my empty wineglass. I was just fine with the other stuff about life and the meaning of the universe. This sentimental stuff is bringing down my mood. Too much drama in the emotion department. Can you lighten it up, please?"

Jaden laughed. "Sorry. Here goes."

Without the aid of a book, he told her a very dirty Irish limerick. The tale made her blush and left her giggling, too. "Now that's more like it," she complimented. "That other stuff is a downer. The poet needs to go to therapy," she joked. "Who wrote that stuff?"

"Me." Jaden slid his book of poetry over to her.

Denise wished that she were an action figure so

that she could morph her body into a background piece of furniture and hide for the foreseeable future. "I'm sorry." Her face felt hot from the shame of her big mouth. "I did think that it was beautiful." She tried to sound sincere. Maybe there were redeeming qualities about the poem. But her inexperience didn't make her a good critic.

"Don't worry, you didn't hurt my feelings. I'm a bit of a corny type." He snapped the book closed. "Guess I was getting too cocky with my poetry selection."

"Corny is good." Denise walked over to Jaden's chair and settled on the arm. "Corny is safe." She played with his hair, tracing the outline of the shape trimmed around his forehead and sideburns. "Corny is sexy."

"You were doing well up to that point. Now I know that you're making fun of me."

"No, not at all," Denise said, but an unwelcoming laugh broke through and she couldn't stop.

"See, there you go."

"I'm not laughing at you. I'm trying to imagine this studious boy making great grades in science and math on his path to engineering, opting for the occasional poetry class. You're a successful, high-profile general contractor, a great mixture of math and science with creative writing. Although I have to admit that your poems also have an underlying dark theme to them."

Jaden had gotten up and headed for the kitchen.

He emerged with slices of apples, pears and cheese. "Sorry for the bad manners. I should've offered you this much earlier."

Denise helped herself to the fruit. After taking a bite of the pear, she opted for more. "Tell me about the poem. Were you talking about the same woman in all of them?"

"I wrote whatever came to mind. Sometimes I used a person for a frame of reference and then I added layers of characteristics to create a flavor. Kind of like a recipe."

"From what you wrote, I'd say that recipe has a good dose of bitters."

Jaden nodded. "You're not off the mark. My father could've done without the poetry sessions. An athlete for a son was his dream. He didn't think there was space for the two to coexist."

"What about your brother?" Denise asked. "Did he follow through with your father's dreams, too?"

"He did try but unfortunately ended his career abruptly with an emotional breakdown."

Suddenly a loud thud sounded overhead. Denise jumped from the chair, almost falling in her attempt to find a safe spot in the room. Her heart pounded in her chest. She looked over at Jaden still seated in his chair. He stared up at the ceiling as if the source of the noise could be seen.

He put his finger to his lips, signaling her to be quiet. She didn't need to be told. Her pulse had slowed down but she was still jittery. He carefully eased himself out of the chair. Each step he took was methodical and almost soundless. Denise refused to remain behind, although she didn't relish acting like a heroine, either. Sticking close to him, she followed, but she didn't have his graceful stealth. Their position must have been given away when she tripped over her feet on the hardwood floor.

Another thud sounded. Louder and closer.

Denise gripped the back of Jaden's arm. She was a nervous mess but not too scared to notice the strength and muscle definition in his arm. She slipped her hand around his forearm, making sure that he took her wherever he went.

"Is someone up there?" Denise whispered. She prayed that he would mention the presence of a lively dog that she'd yet to meet to clarify this mystery.

"No." Jaden slid his arm away from her, motioning that she should remain behind. He grabbed a knife from the fruit and cheese plate.

She thought about arguing with him. But the farther down the hall they moved, the more she wanted to head in the opposite direction. "You go. Shout if you need me to call 911."

Jaden gave her a thumbs-up. Maybe having a

woman in the house made him do stupid things like risk his life to investigate strange noises in his house. He'd much rather take Denise by the hand and leave. No need to play the hero.

He looked behind him. Denise's eyes were round and alert with fear. Too late, he had to continue his task. He paused at the bottom of the stairs, breathing deeply to calm himself. Only when he was ready did he draw on patience to mount the stairs—slowly.

Before he could reach the top, a familiar figure in a distinctively drunken state appeared at the top of the steps. Jaden blinked, hoping he had had some brain miscue. The person grinned, waving down at them. His younger brother, Calvin, always had the worst timing.

"Yo, big brother, where are the bedsheets? I was searching for 'em. You got too many closets. Couldn't find a darn thing." His brother scratched his groin. "Too many rooms. Too much space for one man, if you ask me." He swayed at the top of the steps, as if challenging the probability that if he leaned forward far enough he'd crash headfirst down to the floor.

"Calvin, I didn't know you were coming over tonight." Jaden walked slowly up the stairs. His brother teetering forward then backward unnerved him. He'd have to coax him in a soft voice to take control of the situation. His trepidation at finding an intruder had been replaced with anger at his brother.

He really wished that Denise didn't have to witness this ugliness. There was no way to neatly tuck away this unsavory scene. As the effects of the alcohol seemed to hang off his brother's frame, making him aggressive, the opposite effect occurred in Jaden. Shame and embarrassment settled over his shoulders, weighing on him like an oversize cloak.

He didn't want to look over his shoulder for Denise's reaction. Where he stood midway on the staircase, he heard her move out from her hiding place below when Calvin made his untimely appearance.

Denise sensed Jaden's displeasure, quite understandably. A drunken brother was one thing. A drunken brother in front of a woman he was trying to impress was quite another.

She cleared her throat. "I'll get some coffee going," she offered. She repeated the offer a tad louder when Jaden didn't respond.

"Coffee sounds great, you pretty thing. Where'd you get her, Jay?"

Denise left before she had to hear Jaden's response. She only hoped that his brother didn't take a tumble. A drunken emergency-room patient would be even more problematic.

"Hello, young lady," Calvin yelled from the stairs. "What's your name? Jaden won't tell me."

From the kitchen Denise waited for Jaden to answer. But apparently he chose to ignore his brother. Denise couldn't boast such stamina. She desperately wanted his brother to stop shouting. She stuck her head into view. "It's Denise."

"Coffee smells delicious, Dee Dee." Calvin half walked, half slipped descending the stairs. He continued stumbling across the floor, aiming for the nearest dining-room chair with his arms outstretched zombie-style until he could grip the solid back of the chair with his hands. Small beads of sweat popped onto his brow, which he wiped away with his arm.

From where she stood Denise smelled the foul odor of alcohol and musty sweat. She pushed aside her revulsion for Jaden's benefit. He couldn't look more miserable.

"Sorry about that," Jaden apologized, hovering near his brother until he settled into the chair. His dark, thunderous gaze fastened on his brother.

"Hey, stop apologizing. I'm a big girl." Denise poured a big mug of strong black coffee and added a scant amount of sugar. She didn't think that Jaden would make him leave so inebriated, but the coffee might settle him down for the night. She set the steaming brew on the table.

Jaden stared at his brother, pushing the coffee mug toward him. "I think it's time for you to head to bed, Calvin."

"Sure. You have a date, I see. She'd better treat you right. Right. Right! Right!" Calvin screamed the word repeatedly. His emotional state had no consistency. One second he was a quiet drunk. In a snap, he turned into a belligerent rogue.

Jaden held his brother's hand as he maneuvered the mug to his face. The process was slow because of the hot beverage. Yet he patiently helped his brother until he had drained the cup. A loud belch erupted from Calvin, whose eyes were closing and opening in shorter intervals.

"I'll be right back." Jaden tilted his head toward the stairs.

Denise nodded. She debated helping but figured she'd be more of a burden. In her life she had encountered many things, but alcoholism wasn't one. Witnessing the effects of alcohol scared her.

The loss of control and self-respect did not leave for a pretty sight, not to mention the physical devastation. Calvin's face bore little resemblance to Jaden's. His uneven complexion and loose muscle control had turned his face into a mask.

"Dee Dee, I like you. No, I love you." He gave her a lopsided grin. "Don't let Charlene scare you away, though. She's like a snake in the grass." Calvin promptly started hissing. He moved his hand through the air. "Their little boy is special, you know."

"Enough, Calvin." Jaden propelled him by the arm to the stairs.

Denise had busied herself with making her own cup of coffee. However, she heard every grunt of Jaden's progress with his brother and Calvin's words hit her ears with perfect clarity.

She laid the spoon down beside the coffee mug. Calvin may be drunk, but that didn't mean he couldn't speak the truth. What was more obvious was that Jaden didn't deny or offer an explanation.

Denise kept her hands wrapped around the mug for its warmth. There was another woman. He'd alluded to her, but she hadn't thought it had gone beyond a bad relationship. Now the mention of a boy, his son, unnerved her. He hadn't talked about him. There were no pictures of him. Not even pictures stuck on the refrigerator like most parents had.

"Don't overreact," she whispered to herself. As more minutes flitted by, she imagined all sorts of unsavory things. She drained her mug and set it down on the counter. This evening had nose-dived into drama and she was merely hanging on by her fingers.

"Denise!"

Denise jumped at the sound of her name shouted

from above. Casting her hesitation aside, she ran out of the kitchen. Jaden's call bordered on panic.

"He's just been sick on the staircase and has passed out. He's deadweight. I don't think I can manage safely. Can you help me get him into the guest room?"

She nodded and stepped forward to fit her body under Calvin's arm. His head hung limply to the side, an animallike snore rumbled up through his body and drool oozed out of his open mouth. The smell of his vomit momentarily overpowered her. She gritted her teeth and focused on the task.

Together they dragged and tugged his heavy body up the stairs, stopping a few times to catch their breaths. Finally, Calvin was stretched out across the bed in a spare bedroom. Denise looked down at his sleeping form. Jaden's brother should awaken with a monster headache and a whole lot of appreciation that someone had watched his back.

Although she no longer held Calvin, his odor had worked its way into her clothes. She wanted to get off the clothes and take a long shower. Maybe she could wash away the shock of Jaden's fatherhood.

"I guess you'll be leaving now," Jaden said, his tone soft and flat.

"Let's clean up the stairs first. That smell is going

to be hard to manage." She noted that he hadn't addressed Calvin's comments. Well, she wasn't going anywhere until he talked.

"Thanks."

Together they made the task much easier and faster. Denise truly didn't mind helping. She only hoped that Jaden wouldn't stay aloof with his thoughts. Although she didn't think that he was giving her the brush-off, she recognized that he wanted to ignore the evening's events.

"Well, I think we're done." Jaden wiped his forehead. "Here, let me take those." He reached for the sponge and various cleansers they had used to protect the floor and stair runner carpet. "You can wash up in the bathroom over there."

Denise followed his directions. She washed her hands up to her forearms. Her hair had fallen limp around her face. Her lipstick had worn off, probably before Calvin. The rest of the makeup gave her a ghoulish look. She wadded toilet paper around her fingers, then moistened it with water and wiped away most of the foundation.

The refreshing coolness of the water improved her mood a little. The smell of Calvin had diminished and warred with the smell of the hand soap. Now she was ready to battle with Jaden. Since he wanted to pretend that his brother hadn't delivered a shocking blow, he was about to deal with her anger. She opened the door with attitude.

"I'm not going anywhere, Jaden." She moved in front of him to block his retreat. "I'm trying not to judge you. But things have been pretty tripped out tonight. And you *could* give me an explanation." Her fingers nervously picked at the bracelet on her wrist.

"Charlene was... We had a relationship." Jaden's face twisted in distaste. "She used me. She stole then lied. She's out of my life." Jaden sidestepped her and headed for the bookcase. He pulled another book out from the shelves. His fingers riffled through the pages and then he pulled out a photograph. "I keep him next to this poem about a guardian angel." He held out the photograph, waiting for her approach.

Denise took the photo. Her hand shook a little. She expected to see a child who looked like Jaden, his pride and joy. Instead, she saw a child of mixed parentage. She guessed he was about three years old. His face was upturned toward the camera. She saw the distinctive features of Down syndrome. Over the top of the photograph, she looked at Jaden.

"Please withhold judgment." He took the photograph and kept it in his hand. "I feel low as it is."

"Why?" His admission shocked her. "Do you feel guilty about this little boy?" She added, "He looks like a very sweet child."

Jaden smiled as he looked at the photo. "Yep. He's quite sharp. His mother used him to get to me. And as much as it pained me, I had to put distance between me and them. She was out of control."

"You miss him." Denise had her own guilt for prejudging Jaden.

"Yes, I do. Charlene accused me of rejecting her because of *her* son. He's not mine, but I cared for him like he was. I was so afraid of Demetrius sensing any such thing from me that I stayed in the relationship longer than was healthy."

"Do you think that you'll see him again? Maybe in a few years?" Denise didn't have to gain entry into Jaden's heart to know that he was in pain over this boy.

"I want to see him. But I dare not get too close to Charlene."

"Did you ever love her?"

"No!"

Denise heard too much anger in his tone. Her question might not have been fair. There had to be something that had drawn him to Charlene.

Now they stood facing each other, their conversation stilted. She squeezed the keys in her hand to shake off the dangerous area where her mind wandered.

"I want to stay."

"What?" Jaden shook his head. "I think it's better

if you leave." His gaze shifted upward, his face a worried mask.

"There you go again. Your mind is always in the gutter. You're fine and all that, but I'm not staying to jump in the sack with you." Denise elbowed him in the rib. "Figured you'll need help with Calvin in the morning."

"But what about work? Clothes? Toothbrush?"

"Stop. Thank you for the concern. I'll leave early and head home to clean up. I promise not to show up on the job with morning breath."

Jaden turned into the conscientious host, grabbing fresh linen and towels, and he managed to produce a new toothbrush. "My cleaning service creates houseguest welcome packets as a bonus for my hefty monthly bill."

Denise held up the toothbrush. "Just for this they've earned their money."

"You have your choice of a bedroom upstairs or one downstairs."

"I'll stick to downstairs." Although she would be here to help Jaden with Calvin, she suspected that once his brother was conscious, they might have an uncivil moment upstairs.

Jaden showed her to the room, pointing out the door to the bathroom. He launched into a discourse about the room and the design. Denise didn't care about any of that. Her mind remained occupied with her startling, brazen request to stay with Jaden. At least the twin bed didn't invite any wild rolling around.

Now he'd moved on to the tub and the fact that he had imported it from Italy. Denise smothered a yawn and joined him in the bathroom. The room wasn't extravagantly oversize or opulent. As far as she was concerned, the requisite shower, tub and toilet were in place.

"Jaden, I have to get some sleep." She pushed him out of the bathroom. If he wasn't going to cop a feel or hug her and whisper sweet nothings in her ear, then he had to go.

"Sorry, I get carried away. The place was really run-down when I bought it. The price was a steal. I gutted the interior and slowly rebuilt each room." His face reflected his pride as he inspected various details.

Denise shoved him toward the door. She'd be sure to return the favor by bringing him on her work turf to show him Chicago's underground pipes with all the pleasure that he exuded. But right now, she was beat.

Jaden allowed her to push him toward the door. Then he spun to face her. He stared at her, his tongue finally silent. He took a deep breath. "Looks like we won't have an ordinary friendship." A small smile tugged at his lips. "That is, if you'll be my friend."

"Try to stop me."

"I'll be right upstairs if you need me." His eyes dropped to her mouth that had uttered the challenge in a husky whisper.

"And I'll be right down here, if you need me."

His body responded as if she were its conductor. "Dangerous to walk in the dark."

"Leave a light on in the kitchen to help you…or me." She winked.

"I'm really glad you stayed." He leaned forward and kissed her on her cheek.

Denise closed the door behind him, a huge grin on her face. She was glad that she stayed, too. Sometimes her impulsive behavior didn't always blow up in her face.

Minutes later as she lay in the dark, she toyed with the idea of helping Jaden see Demetrius again. His concern for this special boy touched her more than anything else he could have said.

Chapter 4

Denise entered her office about an hour late. She needed a strong cup of coffee before having to face any employee issues. Her secretary's quick footsteps dogged her the minute she passed the cubicle. As long as Sandy didn't start talking before Denise could drown herself in caffeine, she would be ecstatic.

She entered her office. Immediately the smell of freshly brewed coffee hit her. A soft sigh escaped. "Sandy, you're the best."

She'd bought a small coffee machine for her office. Her daily dosage bordered on toxic. The dark brew kept her going, especially with the long hours and highly stressful job duties.

"Ms. Dixon, I have a message for you from the mayor's office."

"What is it?" She dropped her laptop case onto her desk and pulled out the coffeemaker that seemed permanently attached to her hand. "Well, what are you waiting on?" Sometimes Sandy seemed too hesitant. She needed to show more confidence.

"Um, your blouse is inside out."

Denise looked down at her clothes and groaned. How many people had noticed? Her strict work ethic and stern management style didn't earn her a "favorite boss" title. Her clothing faux pas would be the break-room gossip. As far she was concerned, the error only proved that she was not a morning person.

"I'll close the door so you can change."

Denise quickly fixed her wardrobe, taking the private moment also to fix her hair and retouch her lipstick. "Sandy, come back in, please."

Her secretary's approving grin let Denise know that she was fine again. "The mayor is having a reception on Friday evening."

"Guess I can make it." Denise hated giving up her evening to hobnob with politicians, especially on a Friday.

"You have another conflict. Actually, it starts

later but it means that you'll be running from one to the other."

Denise tried to remember what could possibly be on her calendar. Rarely was it free of engagements. As a matter of fact, she was hoping that it could be cleared to spend the evening with Jaden. His good-bye kiss when she had left was a good sign.

"Your parents' fund-raiser for the family foundation is on your calendar."

Denise groaned. Now she remembered. Not only was it another one of her parents' charitable events, but she had to be the host. There was no way that she could get out of it. The role rotated among her siblings. They wouldn't take kindly to her trying to get out of it.

Sandy cleared her throat. "What do you want me to tell the mayor?"

"What else can I tell him? Yes. I'll be there." Her hectic schedule required fancy footwork to hit the myriad of events and appearances.

Her phone rang and Sandy hurried out the office to get it.

Her intercom buzzed. "Yes?"

"It's a Mr. Bond."

"One second." Denise slipped around the desk and hurried to her door. She closed it and ran back to the phone. "Put him through." Her mood lightened considerably. He'd called before she had broken down and contacted him. "Denise Dixon speaking." She wondered if he sensed the deep smile on her face.

"How are you feeling?" His voice stroked her with sweet gentleness.

"Fine. I had no problem coming in. Got in early and delved right into work," she lied in an upbeat, light voice. She slid down into her chair and swiveled from side to side. "Did Calvin eventually get up?" She'd tried to wait until he awoke, in case Jaden needed her help. But his brother was like a dead log, not budging at their calls.

"He's up with a monster-size hangover. He vaguely remembers you but definitely doesn't recall anything that was said."

Denise heard the tension in Jaden's voice. From the small space of time that she had spent with him, she knew that his brother's shortcomings affected him. She imagined that the morning was strained and uncomfortable for them.

"I called him a taxi and sent him on his way. I think he needs help, but until he decides to change, there's not much any of us can do."

Denise bit back her retort, not wanting to insert herself in his family issues.

"I sound coldhearted."

"I understand." Denise flipped a pen through her

fingers. She wanted to prompt him that he'd called her. Obviously he wanted something.

"I'm heading over to your house. Landscapers are coming to work on the back."

"Is the deck finished?" Denise had stayed away from the property to give Jaden his space to work. Now that they had reached the tail end of the list of projects, her excitement stirred again.

"Yes, the deck is done. By the weekend, you could move in a few items. I may be able to get a few of my men to help if you need it."

"Great news. But I may be looking for your help a little sooner."

"Sure."

"Friday. I have a reception, job related, at the Harvard Club. Interested in accompanying me?"

"I can't make Friday. Sorry."

Denise hadn't expected him to turn her down. She'd assumed that he'd be around. After spending time together impromptu, she'd taken his availability for granted. Not that he couldn't have a life beyond her. "No problem." She paused. "Can we have our drink tomorrow?"

"I would love to but I'm heading out of town tonight and won't be back until Monday. I have another project in Maryland."

Immediately doubts crept in, teasing her with the

thought that Jaden was about to execute a vanishing act. He hadn't previously mentioned going out of town. But the last thing she wanted to do was sound desperate.

"Maybe next week?"

"Maybe," she responded. "Why don't you call me at the beginning of the week? I'll see how my schedule looks. I've got to get back to my work. Have your project manager keep me abreast of developments."

"Sure."

Denise hung up. Her mood had gone south with the news of Jaden's no-show for the remainder of the week. She punched the intercom. "Sandy, I'll be neck deep in work. I don't want to be disturbed for the remainder of the morning."

Denise pulled up her e-mails, which numbered close to one hundred. Most were copies of correspondence from her various bureau heads. Reading each e-mail ate through her time, but in this political environment, she liked to keep tabs on her senior staff. Occasionally she responded with a counterargument, always seeking a different angle on a situation for a fresh solution.

Puzzled that no appointment reminders had popped up on the screen, she double-checked her calendar. Two items were boldfaced in their respective slots. She clicked on one link to find a meeting to discuss future meetings of a task force. She classified that type of meeting as a waste of time. The other meeting dealt with human resources to fill a vacancy. An employee had been recommended for termination.

A knock on the office door interrupted her.

"Yes, Sandy, what is it?"

Her secretary remained in the doorway. In her gray-skirt suit and sensible black pumps, she looked miserable. "I'm sorry, but the man who just called here has called six times. He said that he has to talk to you. He won't take no for an answer." Sandy wrung her hands.

"It's okay, Sandy. Pass the call through." She waited for her phone to ring.

"Yes, Jaden."

"I know you're angry."

"You've lost me there. I'm not sure what you're talking about."

"Our last conversation led me to believe that I had done or said the wrong thing. You ended things with finality."

"Jaden, I'm at work. I try to separate work from play. Playtime is over." She'd treat him like some of her peers who tested her—cool, respectful, reserved. "You're busy. I'm busy."

"I really can't make it. I don't want you to think that I'm giving you the brush-off."

"Sounds like a guilty conscience. Why would I think such a thing?"

"Don't know. Just a vibe."

Denise had to admit that she did feel better now that Jaden had called her back. His intuition was dead-on. But her flash of anger had dissipated when she heard his voice. Letting him off the hook wasn't as big a deal as she pretended.

"We'll get together next week."

"Sure."

Now Denise returned to work in a much better mood. She went through as many e-mails as she could and bought lunch for Sandy as an apology for snapping at her.

Jaden stuffed the cell phone into his pocket and continued on with his inspection of the deck. Denise's house was coming together just as planned and designed. Some projects didn't fare so well. He was glad that he had a dependable crew.

"Jaden, I see you added overhead fans upstairs. It wasn't in the original plans. I'll need to put the wiring in place." Leonard lit a cigarette and inhaled, waiting for a response.

"The owner asked, so I deliver." He looked out at the workers in the backyard but was really casting a keen eye on his friend. "What's got you so worked up? Thought you quit that stuff."

Leonard looked at his cigarette and dropped it

into his cup. Wispy tendrils of smoke escaped through his nostrils. He squinted through the haze. "Susan is having issues. Preeclampsia."

"High blood pressure?" Jaden sucked in his breath. He shuddered to think what his friend and wife were going through.

"She's on bed rest. Everything's stable, baby-wise. But she's distraught. I don't know what to do. Nothing I try seems to be good enough." His friend pulled out another cigarette.

Jaden slowly removed it from his lips.

"Then I brought her mother to stay with us until the baby comes."

"Sounds like you need more than this cigarette." Jaden laughed at Leonard's scowl. "You did good by bringing her mother. She'll calm her better than you can. Doesn't sound fair but it's the law of nature."

"What do you know? You don't have a woman nor a child."

"But I have a mother. And trust me, sometimes that's the only person who can bring peace."

Leonard nodded. "They'll induce in six weeks." He reached into his pocket.

"Here, chew on this." Jaden handed him a stick of gum. "Sometimes I envy you."

"I'll tell Susan you said that, so she can kick your butt."

They laughed.

"Do you think these guys know what they're doing?" Leonard nudged his head toward the landscapers. "Why are they digging up that side of the yard?"

Jaden turned to see what he referred to. "No!" He didn't bother to run down the steps that led to the yard. Instead he hopped over the rail and raced to the men destroying the yard. Behind him, he heard the faint sound of Leonard's laugh.

"Whoo-hoo, one more day of work left." Asia raised her glass in the air, blowing her bangs out of her eyes.

"You all are a bunch of lushes," Denise accused, raising her glass. "I'm drinking a cola, in case any of you try to insult me."

"What's come over you?" Asia prodded. "We haven't heard from you. You missed last month's chapter meeting. You know we have the highway cleanup next Saturday."

"All you do is nag. I took a little break. Didn't know that I had to ask for permission."

"Has anyone heard from Sara or Naomi?" Athena rejoined them after flirting with a man at the bar. She shared very few physical attributes with her twin. Her healthy proportions drew too much male attention, a source of contention between them.

"Naomi is on the road. Sara should be here."

Denise looked at her watch. She looked at her sorority sisters and opted to keep her latest preoccupation to herself. Asia, on the other hand, might spill the news.

"What do you have planned for the weekend?" Asia asked. "I want to go to a club. Care to join me?"

"I'm tired of the club scene." Denise had slowed down on their group treks to the popular nightclub scenes. The girls out and about seemed younger and wore less clothing. So the guys expected all women to act like freaks because of the overly aggressive sexpots who descended on the night scene. They could all have it. Now a good evening was going to a movie, having dinner or a surprise picnic.

They had made pacts to stay together and be a force to be reckoned with after college. But their tastes were developing, along with other interests that didn't include each other. While this reality seemed inevitable, the thought of it scared Denise.

Athena threw her arm around her shoulders. "Sweetie, why the long face? You are dragging us all down. I for one have a lot to celebrate."

"What's up?" her twin asked.

"I've decided to go on a sabbatical. I want to discover and live in other regions of the world."

"You're supposed to be a responsible adult. You can't go backpacking across the U.S." Denise had to set down her glass for this conversation. At no time did she recall Athena entertaining the idea of traveling the world.

"I'm not talking about the U.S." Athena glared at her. "I haven't decided on the place. I haven't decided the date, either. But the timing seems right."

"What about your job?"

"I'm middle management, Asia. I work in corporate banking and there's nowhere for me to go until someone leaves. I'm at the level that gets laid off when times are rough."

"Exactly! That's why you need to hold on to that job for as long as possible." Denise wished that Sara and Naomi were there to help talk some sense into Athena's head. Her sorority sister was always the bohemian of the group. She should have been born a couple of decades earlier and lived her life as a hippie.

"Look, why are you all sweating me? I didn't ask for your guidance. I was simply stating a fact." Athena leaned her head back, ending further discussion.

The conversation meandered through the next hour on lighter topics. The waitress brought refills but they stayed untouched. Again, Denise felt the group disintegrating. She hated the spiraling out-of-control feeling.

"Why don't you come to my parents' fund-raiser tomorrow?" Denise invited. "Come on, ladies. Let's try to be there. We'll have fun all night long."

"Sounds like a plan. I'll work on getting Sara there. Now that Jackson has finally moved in the area on a hunt for their house, we may never see her again. Naomi might be a no-show, too." Asia, her concern still quite visible, looked at her sister.

"Don't think that you'll gang up on me on Friday." Athena crossed her arms. "I know how you women operate. I was the ringleader in many of our plans. I'm wasting my talents in this dead-end job. I want to do this. Some country needs what I can offer."

"And what is that?" Denise didn't mean to sound incredulous.

"I can teach English. Dance."

Denise nodded, but she didn't want to listen. Athena's plan was logical, but roughing it in the United States and roughing it in a poor country were vastly different. This conversation would go nowhere. Athena had that stubborn mask. Denise grabbed her pocketbook. "I have to get a good night's sleep."

"Did you suddenly turn into an old woman?" Asia complained. "Since when have you been the first person to leave? I'm feeling insulted."

"Don't take it personallly." Denise kissed her lightly on the cheek. "I've had a crazy week and it's catching up to me. If I'm going to be up to it tomorrow, I'd better get a good night's sleep."

"Well, this was a sorry happy hour." Asia drained her glass before getting her pocketbook.

"Just because she leaves doesn't mean that you have to leave, too," Athena pleaded.

"Okay, I'll stick around," her sister replied.

Denise slid out of the booth. She did need to head for bed. Slowly she made her way through the growing throng of young professionals that made their daily pilgrimage to the bar. A few men tried to make conversation, but she had no desire to play along.

On the way home, she stopped for a pint of ice cream. Nothing like adding on a few pounds before bedtime. Maybe she'd feel inspired to box up the last of her personal items. The movers were scheduled to arrive early on Saturday to move her into her new house. Thinking about the house reminded her that she hadn't called her father, a daily ritual that she did when she got to work.

"Hello?" She expected to hear her father's voice. Instead, her mother had answered. "Where's Dad?"

"He's away on business. Anything wrong?"

"No." Denise's finger hovered over the off button. "I'll call him on his cell phone."

"Wait, Denise. I haven't heard from you recently. Is everything fine?"

"Yes."

"You're all set for tomorrow? You should show up an hour or so early to run through your lines."

"I told your people not to have me read a dissertation." Denise admired her parents' vision to have a foundation but, with everything else, the responsibilities were sometimes too much. Her sister, Thea, made the foundation her life. However, Denise needed her day job as a reprieve to have her own life.

"They've listened. I got to see the script. It's fantastic."

Denise bit her lip, trying to remain civil to her mother. The more her mother spoke, the less she felt inclined to cooperate. "Mom, I've got to run."

"Good to hear from you. Looking forward to hanging out with you tomorrow."

"Dad isn't coming tomorrow?"

"No, honey. He's in London on business. He's gone for two weeks."

Denise hated not being able to talk to her father. "Could you let him know that I called?"

"Sure. By the way, have you gone to the house recently?"

"Yes." Denise turned into her apartment parking lot. She adjusted her earpiece and grabbed her laptop.

"Do you like it?"

"Yes, Mom. I've told you that I like it."

"Okay, dear. I wish you would come over for dinner one of these days. It's a bit lonely without you."

Her mother's not-so-subtle pressure was duly noted but didn't sway her. She had no desire to visit. Her father would have to be in attendance to be a buffer. Sometimes he tried to defuse their mini-explosions as mediator. But how could he mediate a situation that he didn't understand?

"I love you, sweetie."

"Me, too. Got to go." She clicked off the phone, not wanting to drag the conversation until there was no longer any life in it.

She entered her apartment and dropped her briefcase near the door. Her clothes outlined a path as she stripped. The day had been interminable with more drama than she could handle. She hopped into the shower and let the hot water do its work.

By the time for the mayor's reception had arrived, Denise wished that she could go home, or anywhere else for that matter. A day filled with meetings, visiting job sites and hearing the news about a mishap in her new backyard hadn't put her in the right frame of mind.

The biggest reason for her foul temper had to do with a sexy man who was missing in action. Jaden hadn't called. He hadn't promised to do so but she still expected that he would call. That's what couples did in that first blissful stage.

But she wasn't sure what stage they were in. And by the time he returned, she might not care.

Denise completed dressing in her office. After she'd finished the higher priority items on her desk, she only had forty minutes to get the reception. Once again she earned the honor of being the last person to head out of the office. She greeted the office cleaning crew, as she was already on a first name basis with a few of them.

While she was driving to the mayor's event, her cell phone rang. She eagerly reached for it in her pocketbook. "Hello?"

"Wanted to let you know that we'll be late to the charity event," Asia said.

"Whenever you can make it is fine." Denise ended the call.

She pulled up in front of the hotel and handed the keys to the valet. Other business colleagues had arrived and she hurried to catch up with them.

"Denise, you're looking quite the supermodel tonight."

"Don't even start, Chuck. I have another function to attend after this reception."

"You know, maybe I should be hanging out with you."

Denise offered a watered-down smile. Chuck had made the rounds through many of the women. Thank goodness she'd never gotten to that desperate point. Mutual attraction never occurred between them. If Chuck were honest, and that would be a stretch, he'd have to admit that he wasn't attracted to her. Denise suspected that it was her family's wealth that drew him to her.

As soon as they had checked in at the registration table and received their name tags, Denise excused herself and entered the crowd.

She opted for water as her beverage of choice, considering her role as hostess. Besides, committing social gaffes in this predatory environment could ruin her career faster than she could blink.

Councilman Higgins approached. His sharp eyes bored into her. "How's that big project in front of the hospital?"

"We've brought in a brand-new contractor. His specialty is relining the pipes and he can stay within our budgeted framework."

"Good to hear. I'll want a full report at the next council meeting."

Denise nodded, although the councilman had already turned his back. Now that the project had been forced into the forefront of her thoughts, she decided to text a message to the supervisor assigned to the case.

"You look like an addict."

"Hey, girl, Higgins was just on the trail." Denise barely glanced up at Patricia, her coworker buddy.

"Been there with him and that's why I decided I'd go into the private sector."

"I know he must miss you. You kept him on the ball. His new chief of staff isn't the sharpest tool." Denise shared a disgusted look with Patricia. She really did miss having her around for the occasional rants.

"He wanted to act like I was an indentured servant or something. Now I'm happy, get paid well and I don't have to beg for time off." Patricia held out her left hand and cleared her throat.

Denise looked down at her manicured hand. Her gaze went from the bracelet that looked like tiny ice chips glittering under the lights to the pebble-size diamond on her finger. "Get out of here. You're engaged?"

"Yes!" Patricia threw her arms around her.

Denise hugged Patricia, stepped back to take in her giddy excitement, before hugging her again. When Patricia had left the government to work in the private sector, she had just met a guy and fallen headlong into love.

Patricia's delighted giggles drew attention. The other women who couldn't resist the pull on their curiosity drifted over.

In short time, Patricia had a reception line as if she were visiting royalty. Denise stepped away, truly happy for her friend. Now she was the last one left in the single lane. Their quest to be career-minded women heading to the top of the ladder had been diluted with romance.

Falling in love might be involuntary, but Denise didn't believe that the emotional state was automatic. She liked to have her fun, like her impulses and sexual fantasies with Jaden. But to step into a commitment, opening herself to a risky outcome, had the power to make her shiver.

She looked at her phone to divert her attention from the minicelebration behind her. Maybe Jaden had called. Instead, the only unread message was from her supervisor, and there certainly were no calls that had come in. Disappointment crept in, much to her annoyance, setting her defenses on alert. So what if he didn't call. Jaden Bond was a physical distraction, nothing more.

By the time the mayor began his speech, Denise had a steady e-mail stream about the project. The contractor had dug in the area and punctured a cable line. The hospital had lost some power but thankfully their generators had kicked in. Now the basement had a small leak as the pipe was backed up.

Denise felt the knot in her stomach get tighter. She

tried to look among the crowd to see if Councilman Higgins was getting any advance news about the latest crisis. She finally spied him toward the front, where he stood enthralled with the mayor's speech. Right now the mayor was paying him a compliment. Higgins chest puffed up from the public accolades for his involvement in the mayor's pet project.

Perfect time to ease out of the crowd. She stood on the side of the room for a few more minutes, then slipped out a side door. She had to hurry.

Denise stepped through the doorway of the Grant-Hudson Ballroom, out of breath.

As she walked through the room, she barely touched cheeks with acquaintances and shook hands with those who wanted the opportunity to sell the finer qualities of their charity fund-raising projects. A glance around the room let her know that her sorors hadn't shown up as yet.

"Denise, I'm glad you finally made it." Her younger sister, Thea, approached, looking like a drill sergeant.

With her black, double-breasted pantsuit, gelled hair in an unforgiving ponytail and stylish black pumps, Denise thought Thea looked like a dominatrix. A term she'd called her sister many times over the years in order to start a fight.

"It would look that way." Denise took a couple of

steps back; Thea had a habit of standing toe to toe. Her sister took great pains to challenge Denise's authority. Thea used her height, towering at least four inches above Denise, to make her point. At one time, hair tugging or arms moving like windmills to deliver slaps and punches were their after-school activities. Their childhood physical spats had matured over the years into intellectual challenges, because Thea loved to debate. Denise would've rather just kicked her butt.

"Do you have the script?"

"Yes," Denise answered with confidence, but still patted her pockets for security.

"Well, there is a major change. The president of the abuse center is here and we want him to be recognized."

Denise pulled out her index cards.

"What the heck are those?" Thea snatched the cards from her. "These are handwritten."

"I know. I rewrote them so I can read them in a certain way."

"This isn't a comedy routine." Thea read the card out loud. "I know this wasn't written in this slang. What are you thinking? Look at the people around you. These are not people from the 'hood."

"What the heck would you know about the 'hood? And exactly what is 'hood language? You've grown up with more than a silver spoon."

"Keep it down, both of you." Their mother stepped

between them. She pushed Thea back and then turned her angry attention to Denise. "You need to be in position. We'll begin in five minutes." She kissed her cheek. "Good to see you." Perfectly accessorized and fashionably dressed, her mother epitomized perfection.

Thea, a visual copy of their mother, merely huffed and walked away.

"What's her problem?" Denise was quite ready to drop the issue. Her sister's snobbery irritated her. The seven-year gap in their ages felt as wide as the Grand Canyon. They'd grown up in different times. She had experienced life before the family had prospered, when her parents were married. Meanwhile, since her mother remarried to their father, Thea and her brother had always enjoyed an upper-crust lifestyle. But Denise had no hang-ups over her stepfather. When her own father had disappeared from her life, her stepdad remained constant. His love extended to her with no reservations. Her mother warned him of spoiling all the kids, especially her, but he never listened.

"Your sister is very serious about all of this."

"Oh, I get it. Because I have a job with the great unwashed, I'm not dedicated. I'm not a true emptyheaded socialite."

"Denise, please, stop fighting." Her mother took

her hand and led her to the stage. "You know, sweetheart, it's not you against the world."

Denise pulled her hand away. "I'm ready."

Her mother studied her for a few seconds. "We used to be alike, you and me." She placed her hand against her daughter's cheek.

Denise turned her head slightly. She read the pain in her mother's eyes, but it was quickly hidden behind a bright smile.

"Looks like the Browns have just arrived." Her mother reached out to touch her but then dropped her hand.

Twinges of guilt nettled her. Denise took a deep, steadying breath. The thought that they were alike wasn't acceptable to her. She wished her father were here. His presence would be comforting and nonjudgmental.

Across the room, the event planner waved at her. Guess it was time to start this circus. Time to do her job.

An hour later, she'd wrapped up the portion of the event when they distributed awards, begged for more money and honored the accomplishments of the foundation. Denise was proud of her family's legacy, despite her heated moments with Thea. Her brother, Nate, missed most of these moments, since he was the adventurer off on a safari in Africa. His playboy, devil-may-care attitude amused her. His many colorful stories made her envy his spirit and freedom.

She ordered a lemon drop, enjoying the sugar-crusted rim of her glass. The casino-style theme certainly helped their patrons to part with their wealth. She'd been in that frame of mind many times and had gotten into serious debt. Her sorors and her father had bailed her out. She didn't want to see that hiccup as anything beyond a difficult moment in her life.

Cheers erupted at certain tables as people celebrated their winnings. The games of chance pulled her attention. Denise surrendered and walked over to the blackjack table.

The longer she stayed at the table, the more she wanted to play. The craving grew stronger, like an adrenaline rush. Her sorors hadn't arrived. And if she had a boyfriend, well, he wasn't there, either. She was standing in the middle of this noisy room having a one-person pity party.

"Hey, I want in." She took a seat at the blackjack table. Her pulse sped. Her mouth watered. The sound of the chips being stacked, the dealer's fingers pulling out cards and the players demanding to be hit were like tunes in an orchestra that was about to play a symphony.

And she played. Her stack increased and decreased, mostly decreasing as time passed. She rationalized that it was all for a good cause as she bought hundreds of dollars' worth of chips.

"Denise, don't you think you should take it easy?" Her mother stood behind her chair.

"I must learn that trick." Denise pushed three stacks forward.

"What are you talking about?"

"Keeping the worry only in your eyes while the rest of your face looks like a mannequin." Denise winced when the dealer pulled her stack toward him. "It's all about charity."

"Stop!" Her mother signaled to the dealer to cut her out of the next deal.

Denise shot out of the chair. "I am not a child, Mother."

"I beg to differ. I'm not sure what's gotten into you. It's like you're bent on hurting me."

"Are you sure you want to start something?"

Her mother visibly backed down. She smoothed her clothes. As usual, Thea popped up, her teeth bared. "Why don't you go home?"

Denise's hand clenched into a fist.

"We're here, soror." Asia stood next to her. She slipped a hand around her waist. "Interested in blowing this joint and getting pancakes?"

Denise caught their hint, but didn't feel like stuffing her face. "I'm not done yet."

"Fine. Then we'll all go with you." Athena locked arms with her twin.

Her line sisters, except for Naomi, stood across from her. She could look at all of them but Sara. The condemnation played against her conscience. She felt as if she'd broken a promise.

"Waitress, I'll have a ginger ale." At least when it came to drinking, she could play the good girl. She turned to the roulette wheel. "I'll be here for a little bit."

Sara took the seat next to her. She leaned in until her breath tickled her ear. But there was no humor in the action. "You had better fight this demon. We didn't pledge together and overcome all the odds for you to take the cowardly way out."

Denise took the dice off the table and rolled them around in her hands. The small, harmless token had a crippling power that wormed its way into her soul and settled there. But all she had to do was put down the dice and back away from the table.

Thea had taken her mother away. They would probably talk about her and how terrible she was. She didn't care what they had to say. The wall that she'd erected to block her emotions had gotten thick over time.

But her sorors stayed, not budging an inch.

"Denise!"

Denise turned toward the sound of the familiar,

sexy voice. He looked completely out of place in his casual shirt and dark blue jeans. He stood with his fingers hooked in his pockets. He looked fantastic among the tuxedoes and designer suits.

Her sorors had the good sense to break their wall of solidarity and let her through. She took two slow steps toward him. Then he smiled and her restraint snapped.

Before cold reality could ruin her sudden giddiness, she was in his arms. She wrapped her arms around his neck and buried her face in his chest. He was more than a gorgeous man who had unexpectedly shown up. In this knee-deep muck that she had managed to step into, he was the solid pillar for her to hang on to.

"I think that I came at the right time."

"You sure did." She enjoyed his arms still being around her.

"I want to take you out of here."

"You'd better."

"My place?" Jaden asked.

"Do you have a king-size bed?"

"Wasn't planning on using the bed."

"Who said anything about using the bed? That's for after I'm done with you."

Chapter 5

Jaden made the journey to his house in one piece, a minor miracle. He could barely keep his hands off Denise. How could he have thought that he could walk away from her? And he'd tried.

He did have business to conduct, but it wasn't as far away as he'd pretended so he had returned to town early. The euphoric feeling that overcame him whenever he was with Denise, or when he even thought about her, unsettled him. Never had a woman taken control of his mind and emotions. He worked hard to keep life calm and pleasantly predictable. He functioned better that way.

Her entry into his life had hit him like a cyclone, whipping everything into a frenzy. Giving in to his preoccupation, he had acquiesced and sought her at her family's event. He had to battle with the staff at the door because of his casual attire, but he wasn't going to be denied.

"Why so quiet?" Denise touched his leg, a dangerous move.

"Concentrating on not breaking any laws."

"I feel like I'm in a time warp," she teased.

"Look, you're going to have to stop stroking my thigh. I can't concentrate and it's making me drive faster."

"Good. I don't want you to cool down."

Jaden punched the accelerator. He knew the universe was on his side because the traffic lights stayed green as he made his way in record time to his house.

He pulled into the driveway in front of the house instead of parking his prize car in the garage. Tonight he couldn't care less about protecting his sports car from the elements.

Like a caveman, he tossed Denise over his shoulder, pleased at her delighted squeals that pierced the quiet, sleeping neighborhood. He hurried into the house before the security detail could put in an ill-timed appearance.

"If you don't put me down…" Denise giggled.

"Not till I get you inside."

"Stop!" she said, laughing.

Without ceremony, he finally set her down abruptly.

"Please tell me that you didn't bring me to the bathroom." She stopped short at the shower. "I'm willing to try a lot of stuff, but not the floor of a bathroom." She headed to the door.

"Still seeing me as a person with no class, huh?" Jaden removed his shirt then unbuckled his belt.

"I smell chlorine." Denise walked toward a glass door. She pushed it open. "Oh, my. You've got a pool. You didn't show me this before!"

"I wanted it to be a surprise for later on," he explained.

Jaden pulled off his pants. Denise's bemusement had him chuckling, but she would either join him in disrobing or he would toss her into the pool with her clothes on.

"But I can't go out there."

"You can't swim?" He'd never thought of that.

"I can swim but what about my hair?"

"I hate to tell you but your do is half done." Jaden walked over and gently pulled down her upswept hair. He wanted her. And a hairstyle wasn't going to stand in his way.

"I'm too into you at this moment," Denise said. "Otherwise, I'd beat you with my shoe for manhandling my hair." She stepped up and kissed him like she owned him.

And he was all hers.

He allowed her to take the lead with her devilish tongue. She kissed him to a titillating peak. Her mouth was soft and full of sensuality. He responded to her ministrations with a hunger that carried the gnawing edges of greed.

"Am I forgiven?" he asked, after he pulled away from the suction of her mouth. "I'm going into the pool. Come join me."

"You're the first man I've known who wants to exercise before he gets busy."

"Increases the stamina."

"For you or for me?"

"Well, we'll see, won't we?" He stood in his briefs, enjoying her admiring gaze roving over his body.

He classified himself as a nerd, but he knew his body was in tip-top shape. He didn't work out and watch his diet just to catch a woman's eye—it was his way of life. He didn't have to contract his muscles to know that he had washboard abs and lean, muscled hips.

"Are you going to shield your eyes?" he asked, with his finger in the waistband of his briefs.

Denise crossed her arms in a defiant pose. "Nope.

You want to get all dramatic, then go ahead and strip under the bright lights."

He slipped off his briefs and tossed them into a chair. "You've got exactly one minute to get into the pool, Miss Dixon. I'll go do a warm-up lap." He turned away and headed for the pool.

But not before Denise checked out his erection.

Denise wanted an award for best actress in a serious, heart-numbing role. Many reactions to Jaden's naked body would have been appropriate. Her least favorite would have been take offense and leave the house. Not only was that not an option, she entertained an entirely opposite reaction.

Plain and simple, she wanted Jaden beyond a simple bump and grind. She wanted to make love with the intensity and tenacity of a student with a 4.0 grade point average. The thought of her fingers massaging his brown skin stirred her appetite.

She took off her jacket, pulled her blouse over her head then peeled off her pants. She was standing in her matching black lace bra-and-panties set and knee-highs, when Jaden reentered the dressing room.

He stood across from her with the water dripping and beading on his body. In her opinion, he wore the water well. Each trickle traced the indentation of a muscle that framed his gorgeous body.

"What's taking you so long?" he asked, striding toward her.

She held out her hands, giggling. "I have to take off my knee-highs."

"From where I'm standing, you need to take off a lot more than that."

She hopped on one foot as she tried to get off a stubborn knee-high. Before she could accomplish the feat, Jaden scooped her up for the second time that evening. He pushed through the door and entered the pool area. She looked up, expecting to see stars, but was pleasantly surprised that the pool was enclosed. The walls of the pool room were beveled glass.

Her admiration came to an end when she realized that Jaden had stopped. Panic started when she looked down and saw that he was holding her over the water.

"Don't you dare," she warned, looking into his dark eyes. "I don't want to be dropped." She wrapped her arms around his neck as a warning to him. However, with her breasts crushed against his chest, she acknowledged her weaker state.

He nuzzled her mouth, playing with her lips. Soft kisses and slow darts of his tongue as it teased the insides of her lips stoked the fire raging in her.

The water lapping at her behind shocked her. Jaden had descended the steps into the pool with her.

As far she was concerned, he had used distracting tactics to get her into the pool.

"Now you've gotten my underwear wet," she teased.

He let go of her, allowing her to stand. Her body rubbed against his, getting used to buoyancy. He tilted her chin so that he could look down into her face. "I promise you that by the time I'm done, they will be dry."

"Oh, really. I guess you'll be tiptoeing in between to the dryer." She was glad that she was in the water. Her body could stay cool despite the flush of excitement, the high anticipation, of what she and Jaden could bring to the surface.

"Allow me." He unsnapped her bra in the front and placed it with care, as if it were a precious gem on the side of the pool.

Now that her breasts were free of the thin barricade, she could feel the water bathing her heated skin and sensitive nipples.

"One second. I'll be right back." Jaden took a deep breath and slipped below the water's surface.

Denise looked down into the water wondering what he was up to. Once he had placed his hands on her hips, she realized that he intended to disrobe her without oxygen. She tried to help but he brushed her hands away.

She held on to the pool's edge for support. His

hands slid down her panties and pushed it down her legs, over her knees to the bottom of the pool. She stepped out of the thin material.

Jaden shot up out of the pool. He sucked in air, breathing normally after a short time. "Be right back."

He disappeared again under the water. Despite his teasing, she had no intention of getting her hair wet and was about to tell him so when he disappeared.

The water's surface distorted the image, but she quite clearly recognized his hand between her legs. He trailed a line from her ankle up to her knee. She bared her teeth in faintly animallike behavior, glad that he couldn't see what she had been reduced to. And then his progress was halted by the roadblock between her legs.

His fingers stroked her, making introductions that didn't require speech. His lips against her body made her arch her back. Her fingers squeezed the unyielding pool's edge. Then his finger entered her, sealing any further introduction. She gritted her teeth and bared down to enjoy more of his finger-talk.

When he came up for air, she kissed him, refusing to let him go. With his finger still deep inside, he kissed her with a savage force that matched her desire. She wrapped her legs around his waist. "I want you so bad."

"I want you, too." He let her go and then pulled himself into the middle of the pool. "Let's swim."

"You're cruel."

"Maybe." He swam effortlessly toward one end of the pool.

Okay, so his foreplay was a little different. She could learn to hang. She pushed off from the edge of the pool and swam toward him and then beyond. She would swim two laps and then demand that he fulfill her needs, or else.

When she was finished, she stepped out of the pool. Enough with the foreplay. "Now you have exactly one minute or I'm coming with or without you."

Jaden didn't need any further incentive. He exited the pool seconds after she did. Walking on the wet tiles made his progress much slower, but he had inspiration.

When Denise emerged from the pool like Venus rising, he thanked her parents for their contribution. She was beyond fine. Her natural beauty was in her lean frame that surrendered to voluptuous hips.

By the time he entered the dressing room, she had stepped into the shower. He smelled shampoo and smiled. He washed off the chlorine in the next shower stall.

"I think we're too clean now to get all dirty again," he said, drying off with a thick bath towel.

"You're the one who wanted a dip in the pool." Denise threw her towel at him. "Let me go hunt for a more practical place."

Jaden followed her, enjoying the sway of her hips as she headed up the stairs. She paused at the top, looking both ways.

"It's to the right," he directed.

"What's to the left?"

"Another master suite. It's never been used."

"Never?"

He saw that he had piqued her interest. "Guess I saved it for a special occasion."

"And there's nothing more special than this?" She turned to face him, a mischievous glint twinkling in her eye.

He kissed her, propelling her down the hallway into the room. The softness of her body tempted him and he didn't mind succumbing. His hand slid up the back of her head as his fingers intertwined with the silky length of her hair.

"Baby, do you have a condom?"

"I'll be back in the blink of an eye." Jaden hurried back down to the dressing room where he kept his protection.

"Back in no time." He kissed her neck. "Did you miss me?"

Denise lay on her back on top of the sheets.

"Thought I'd start without you." Her hand circled one nipple.

Jaden shook his head. "Nope, I'm not sharing, not even with you." He pulled her legs toward him, bringing her close to him. He kissed her breasts, nuzzling them with his face. Her nipples he saved for last, teasing them with the tip of his tongue. Denise arched up to him, sucking air through her teeth.

Her writhing excited him. His hands stroked her body, lingering over the fullness of her buttocks. Touching her drove him wild. After sheathing his sex and cupping her behind, he entered her hard. She gasped and then moaned.

Much more slowly he continued filling her. When she relaxed against him, he started the sensual dance. His rhythmic thrusts carried their own beat that were answered by the gyrations of her hips.

Wherever he led, she followed. Their union was natural and uninhibited. In his arms, Denise didn't back away from all that he offered. This was no time to examine his emotions, yet he set aside his vulnerabilities about the future.

Now. In the present, he wanted to feast on the delights that Denise brought for his consumption. Likewise, he hoped that she enjoyed the same level of satisfaction.

Her legs clamped around his waist with a vicelike

grip that shocked and delighted him. From the tightness on her face and the quivering between his legs, he sensed her readiness.

"Ride with me," she gasped. "Come with me."

Jaden didn't need any further invitation. He gripped her shoulders and bore down. He wanted to feel the electricity that charged between them setting them on the same road, at the same time. He quickened his thrusts, matching the increasing tempo. Their bodies writhed, stretched, pushing toward the hypersonic boom that shattered their thoughts, ripped the breath from their lungs, quickened their pulse to the edge of reason.

With each torturous cry from her lips, Denise raised her hips to grind through Jaden's powerful releases. Her legs trembled from the grip she had sustained. But she welcomed all of Jaden between her legs. Deep within her, the pulsations continued while slowing down so that life was no longer a blur. She could now get off the heady merry-go-round and focus on the real world that stood still.

"I hope I didn't hurt you."

"I hope I didn't wear you out." Denise kissed the tip of Jaden's nose.

"I'm famished." On cue, his stomach rumbled. "I'll slip away and get us some food."

Denise nodded, also reading that Jaden wanted

time to clean up. When he left, she also got up and headed for the bathroom. The bright, cruel light put her in a spotlight in front of the mirror. She shuddered at the sight.

Her hair was disheveled and appeared matted. The rest of her body, well, regardless of how it looked, it felt marvelous. She set about trying to make nice with her hair.

"I brought up your clothes," Jaden called from the bedroom.

Denise stuck out her head. "I'm sending you the bill for my hair and clothes."

"Didn't realize that a heated moment brought out the comedian in you."

"I'd say we had more than a moment."

Denise emerged from the bathroom. This time she tilted his chin to kiss him. His lips responded to her, his hands covered her back. She cupped his face with all the tenderness of holding something precious.

She looked into his eyes. "One more time?"

A long, guttural moan was his only response.

This time under the entrance of the sun beaming into the bedroom, they made love with a lazy abandon. Half starved, half exhausted, they clung to each other and let their bodies move on autopilot.

Denise kept her eyes open, when she could. Other times, the throes of desire hit so hard that she swore her eyes rolled back in her head. But she held on, sinking her fingers into Jaden's back as his hips ground against hers.

Their passion traveled a path together, neither one running ahead of the other. At that destination point that had no definition, no place on a compass, they surrendered to the explosions of their bodies' celebration.

Denise closed her eyes and held on. This was a beautiful storm that she wanted to ride with Jaden. She wished it would never end.

"I think we may need to go to an all-you-can-eat." Denise followed Jaden into the kitchen the next morning.

"I'm too weak to think about driving."

"Oh, my car." She remembered that her car was still at the ballroom.

"We'll get it." He pulled out a frying pan from the cupboard. "After we eat."

Denise wanted something to keep her mind off the past glorious hours. She didn't want to behave like a teen with her first crush. Grown women had to be prepared that there might not be anything beyond an initial physical attraction.

"Why don't you take a seat at the dining-room table?"

"But I wanted to help."

"You're distracting me and I'm hungry. Let me do my thing."

Denise raised her hands in mock surrender.

He whipped up an omelet, pancakes and turkey bacon. He presented her breakfast with freshly brewed coffee.

"You are quite handy. I like a man that is versatile. Thank you." Denise looked at her laden plate. This morning she wasn't counting calories, points or anything else. And she was quite certain that she could eat every crumb of this meal because she had worked up an appetite.

"What time do you want me to help you move?"

"I had forgotten about moving. I appreciate you helping me out with your men. The moving company had a lot of hidden fees. I'm willing to pay them, don't get me wrong, but they were trying to take advantage."

"No need to explain. I understand what you mean. Let's finish up here and I'll organize them."

"I'm excited about moving into the house."

"Good. You had me worried there for a second. You didn't seem to want the house."

"I just wish that I could do more things on my own."

"And I'm sure that you are very independent. But isn't the house a tradition in the family?"

She nodded. Little did he know that she had received her gift as an incentive to stop her gambling habit. In their own way, her parents thought she gambled because she needed money or stability.

"Don't be ashamed of it or who you are."

"I'm not," she retorted. He'd touched a nerve.

"I work with the wealthy and superwealthy on most of my projects. You'd think that would guarantee payment, but they can be the tightest when it comes to giving up their cash."

Denise nodded, understanding that his comment wasn't directed at her.

"All that money messes with your mind," Jaden reflected.

"What makes you the expert? What inner demons are you hiding? 'Cause I got a lot."

Jaden shrugged. "I think we all do."

"Yeah." Denise pushed away from the table and took the dishes into the kitchen. In this perfect world where Jaden behaved like a responsible adult, her weaknesses had no place.

"Last night, when I came to get you…"

Denise set down the dishes in the sink. "Please, I don't want to talk about last night."

"Look, I'm here to help."

Shame flooded her body and her face grew hot from embarrassment. His scrutiny had pierced her armor. She felt naked, and not in the sexual sense. "I don't need anyone's help."

"Looked to me as if your family and friends all wanted to help." Jaden joined her in the kitchen.

All of a sudden, the open, airy room felt the size of one of her closets. She tried to escape past him. His hands grasped her arms, forcing her to remain still. She kept her gaze focused on the embroidered emblem on the left side of his shirt.

"We're friends, remember, and lovers. I think you're trapped in this painful box, suffocating yourself in the process."

"Please don't try to perform therapy on me. What you saw last night was remnants of a family disagreement."

"And is that why Sara wanted you to come away from the tables?"

"Drop it, Jaden." She hadn't meant to raise her voice, but she didn't have the control she would've liked in this situation. "I haven't invited you into my life." She pushed away and ran toward the door to escape from further probing. The realization hit her that she didn't have her car. She stopped at the front door and rested her head against the sturdy barrier. "I want to go home."

He paused a beat. "Not a problem."

The air of excitement was gone during this ride. Denise fastened her gaze out the window. Her other senses were tuned to every movement he made.

I haven't invited you into my life.

How could she have said such a thing? And she knew that her emotional remark had wounded him. His face had registered shock and the unpleasant realization that she'd shoved his act of friendship in his face.

An apology could set things straight. But she couldn't honestly say that it would be sincere. She wanted Jaden and enjoyed being with him. The idea of a future with him intrigued her. But this pit that she'd dug and jumped into with both feet imprisoned her. As long as she could pretend that everything was fine and normal, she didn't have to deal with the feeling of being trapped.

She wanted to keep her lives separate. Last night proved that her wish might not be fulfilled. In the stark reality that came with daylight, she had to deal with her mother, Thea and her sorority sisters.

When Jaden pulled up next to her car, Denise mustered scraps of her courage. She opened the door, a small act that could speed her escape after his reaction. Without looking at him, with her feet on solid ground and her car a couple of steps away, she confessed. "Jaden, I'm a gambler."

Jaden heard the anguish in those words. He reached out to touch her, give her reassurance. She'd slipped out of his car in a rush and jumped into her car. He respected her need to be alone.

Her admission didn't provide any revelation apart
from what he already knew. But it eased the hurt that
she'd inflicted with her caustic words. His insecurity
flared, reminding him that he had stepped right into
another situation of hurt and betrayal.

Yet all the feelings he experienced were too vivid
and powerful for them to be only his gullibility. And
in one swoop, Denise had confirmed his belief with
her admission. He didn't drive away until she had,
and then he returned home.

At noon, most of his men had showed up, glad for
the chance to make some extra cash. He had thought
about his brother, who could probably use the money,
too. Denise had been brave with her demons. He had
set aside his judgment and invited his brother into his
life for a few hours.

Now they were all back at Denise's apartment. "I've
packed everything that I want you to start moving."

Jaden hid his smile as she bossed everyone
around. She looked too sexy in a tank top and jeans.
Once in while, he would catch one of his men giving
her a lingering look as she walked by. "I don't think
she's paying you to watch."

"No, boss."

"Then let's get moving." They could call him
selfish, but he wasn't in the mood to share.

His men had made several trips to the rented truck when his brother finally put in an appearance. Jaden slipped on his shades to hide his irritation. Hopefully his brother hadn't drunk his last meal.

"Calvin, good of you to join us."

"What do you want me to do?" Calvin brushed past him into the apartment.

"Most of the work is already done."

"I have plants in the dining room that still need to be moved." Denise offered her hand. "Nice to see you again."

"Again?" Calvin looked at Jaden.

"You were in my home when Denise was visiting."

Realization came into his expression. "Oh, I wasn't my best then."

"We're not always our best every minute of the day." Denise offered to let him off the hook.

Jaden grunted. Biting back a sarcastic response, he moved away and busied himself with taking down framed prints. He surveyed the area from his perch on the stepladder. His men had cleared the apartment in under an hour.

"I don't want to waste the guys' time," Denise said to Jaden. "Do you think you can handle the remaining items while I head over to the house? My sorors will be meeting me there, too."

"Don't worry about anything. And thank you for

being so honest with me earlier." He placed his arm around her waist and guided her to the front door. "See you in a few minutes." He placed a strategic kiss near her earlobe. "You look good enough to eat."

Denise squirmed out of his grasp. She winked at him and blew a kiss as she headed out of the apartment.

"I think she's in love with you," Calvin said. He placed a phone that had been disconnected from the wall into a box. "Are there more phones?"

Jaden nodded, pointing toward the kitchen where a wall phone was still connected. He tried to ignore Calvin's comment, poking into his private affairs. What would he know about Denise being in love? However, his brother's claim raised a glimmer of hope.

"Do you think you should be leading her on?" Calvin emerged from the kitchen. "Keep it up and you'll have a track record."

Jaden continued to take down the prints. He didn't know why Calvin deliberately irritated him. If he kept it up, he'd cut this arrangement short and not have him go to Denise's house.

"You can't pretend that Charlene and Demetrius don't exist. I saw Charlene the other day when Demetrius was sick. You won't take her calls, and I was there for her. I'm a poor substitute for you, though."

"Stop stirring up what doesn't concern you," Jaden warned. "Charlene is in the past. I love Demetrius, but it won't do any good to be used as a tool by his mother. And you don't need to do anything on my behalf." Jaden walked past his brother to his car and loaded in the prints.

"I forgot, you've got your own thing going on."

"What do you want from me?" Jaden headed back into the apartment. His patience had thinned to almost nothing.

"I'm pissed because you're living your life with your crazy rules, running over people's feelings. You don't care about anything or anyone, you cold-hearted, son of—"

Jaden grabbed Calvin by the collar and pushed him backward until a solid wall deterred his efforts. "Don't lay your paranoid B.S. at my feet. I don't owe you anything. As a matter of fact, I'm tired of picking up after you and propping you up. And with everything that I've done, you don't have an ounce of appreciation. And this obsession you have about Charlene needs to stop. That chapter of my life is closed."

"You're so slick with your lies that you actually believe them. Does Denise know?"

"Thanks to you, yes, she knows."

"And she still wants to be with you?" Calvin pushed his hands away and fixed his shirt. "Don't you find that odd?"

"Find what odd, Calvin?" Jaden rubbed his forehead. "Are you sure you haven't been drinking?"

Calvin launched himself at him. His wild punch glanced off his chin, not enough to do damage, but it stung nevertheless. Jaden's body went rigid with coiled rage. His hands balled into fists and he badly wanted to wipe the smile off Calvin's face.

"I think you need to leave. You came here picking a fight. I'm not going to allow you to take me to that place." He shoved Calvin toward the door.

"I want my money."

Jaden sighed. This unkempt man in front of him was his baby brother.

The thought that his hands were at his baby brother's neck roiled his stomach. The best thing in this case was for them to go their separate ways.

He pulled out his wallet and opened it. "Here's one hundred dollars."

His brother took the money with a nod. He walked over to his latest car. Jaden didn't want to know what had happened to the last one. He stayed until his brother drove off and disappeared from view.

With Calvin gone, the apartment was empty. He gathered the few items that hadn't been boxed. Then he locked the apartment and drove over to Denise's new home.

His phone rang as he pulled up to her house. He

glanced down and saw that his mother was calling. "Hi, Mom."

"Haven't heard from you. How are you doing?"

"Sorry about that. Life got busy."

"Not too busy for you to give me a quick call. Are you coming over for dinner tomorrow? I'm cooking baked chicken. You know we've got to watch your father's cholesterol."

"How's Dad? Is he taking it easy?"

"When I get on his case, he'll rest, but only for a little bit. Your brother is on his mind. But I told him that you were handling it." She paused. "Have you been able to reach out to Calvin?"

Jaden turned off the engine. "I've seen him." He bit his lip, trying to spare his mother from the sordid details. "I gave him money."

His mother clucked her tongue. "I know he needs money, but I don't want you to make it easy for him. He needs a job, to get himself a nice girl and live a decent life. I tried to get him to come to church with me. He needs to unburden his soul."

"Mom, Calvin needs professional help." He could hear the argument about to be delivered. "I'm not saying that Pastor Womack can't help him, but Calvin needs to be in a program."

His mom was silent for a bit. Then she spoke softly, "I've been afraid of that."

Jaden hated to make her worry. His parents should be enjoying their retirement and the results of their hard work and love. Instead they took on the guilt of his brother's condition. He carried that boulder of guilt on his shoulder on a daily basis.

"Promise me you'll get him to come to dinner tomorrow," his mother continued. "I think that it's important we at least act like a family. We can't wait for only birthdays and Christmas."

"I'll try."

"Do more than that, Jaden. I want both of you here tomorrow. I've got to run." His mother hung up.

Jaden got out of the car in a melancholy mood. He grabbed a box and entered the house.

Inside, people moved around completing their tasks. Several large pizzas were lined up on the kitchen counter. Beer stuck randomly throughout filled a cooler packed with ice. Music blared out of speakers, the source unseen.

A party was in full progress. The furniture had been set in place throughout the house. The home had been transformed. He went out on the balcony in search of Denise.

"Hi, Jaden."

"Hi, Sara. Is Denise out there?" He motioned toward the deck where another group was in lively discussion. He suddenly felt left out.

"She's upstairs. First bedroom on the left. But I guess you know that." She wrinkled her nose at him, her mouth quivering with amusement.

"Thanks." Jaden's ears burned, imagining what kind of conversation Denise and Sara had while he was absent. He headed upstairs, dodging boxes that lined the steps and hallway. "Denise?"

Two identical faces popped out at him from the master suite. He walked toward them, sure that he was also the topic of their discussion. Their huge grins and exaggerated assessment of him as he entered the room provided the evidence.

"Jaden, meet Asia and Athena, my sorors. We pledged together." Denise lay on her side across the bed, her hand propping up her head.

Grateful that they didn't dress alike or have similar hairstyles, he shook their hands.

"Did I leave a lot of stuff to clean up at the apartment?"

"I could handle it. I brought three boxes and several of the framed prints."

"I don't know about you, but I'm exhausted."

Jaden nodded. Her sorors unnerved him with their chuckling. He felt as if a neon sign were flashing over his head saying he had made wonderful, glorious love with their line sister.

"Well, we're going now. Sara is ready to go."

"Thanks for coming by, ladies. Make sure everyone leaves with you. I've paid them all." Denise stretched and yawned. She groaned, scrunching her face in pain.

Asia patted him on the arm and left the room.

"Next time, you'd better stretch. Wouldn't want her to suffer a muscle pull." Athena giggled and left.

Jaden moved to the chest of drawers and leaned against it. Denise looked at him with a small smile.

"You're so incredibly sexy standing there, tall, dark and drop-dead gorgeous. You can wear the heck out of a pair of jeans. I love a man with a grabable ass."

"There is no such word."

She swung her legs over the side of the bed and scooted over to him. Then she pulled him to stand between her legs. With a bold, saucy wink as his only warning, she placed her hands on his buttocks and squeezed. "Grabable."

The minute her hands molded around his butt cheeks, Denise wanted more. She looked up at him, melting into the dark pools of his eyes, sending her message through the slight pressure of her fingers. And just in case he didn't understand the urgency, she rubbed her cheek against the bulge in his jeans.

A grin of pure pleasure crossed her face. His arousal acknowledged the personal attention. She planted a kiss in gratitude.

"Don't you want to make sure your guests leave?" Jaden sounded as if he'd been sprinting and had broken a world record.

Denise shook her head. "That adds a certain somethin' somethin'." This time she cupped his arousal, deliberately sabotaging any analysis of the moment.

When he placed his hands on her shoulders to push her back against the bed, she squirmed free. Instead of waiting for him to lavish her body with attention, she wanted to pay homage to his. He'd eventually get what she wanted, to take the lead. But right now, this very minute, with guests calling up the stairs to tell her they were leaving, she wanted to erase the frown she'd seen when he entered the room. She wanted to kiss away the tightness around his lips. She wanted to stroke him into relaxed submission for the moment when she would mount him.

"You're deliciously wicked."

"Not so fast. I've done nothing to get that indictment…yet." Moving off the bed to stand behind him, she pulled his shirt over his head, alternating between kissing and licking in swirls along his back. His frenetic twitching egged her on. She ran her hand up to the back of his head, holding him in place. Her tongue greeted his flesh along his neck, down to his shoulder to the middle valley of his spine.

Jaden's groans had replaced his protests. His

hands reached back for her. She remained elusive, except to move in and bathe his back with her tongue.

"Take off your jeans."

He obeyed.

"Everything. Then lie in the middle."

Again, he obeyed.

She climbed on the bed, standing over him. "I want all of you."

He reached for her leg, but she pushed his hand aside.

"You don't get to touch." She moved off the bed and walked over to her dresser. She removed four scarves from her dresser and returned to Jaden.

"May I?" She snapped a scarf taut between her hands.

Alarm showed on his face. But then he relaxed and nodded.

Denise tied each wrist and ankle to the corners of the head- and footboards.

"Is this some sort of test?"

"You could say that." Denise hadn't orchestrated any of this; instead she was going with whatever her body craved. What she was about to do was more of a test for her than Jaden. Could she mute her analytical tendencies for pure decadent joy?

She pulled the curtains, softening the harsh light. Although the rest of her boxes hadn't been unpacked, her mood candles had been the first things to be found and placed in her bedroom. Now, she lit the various clusters of candles.

In the soft shadows of the room, she undressed, not going out of her way to allow Jaden to witness her disrobing. He craned his neck to help his vantage point, but had to drop his head back onto the bed when the effort proved to be futile.

Naked, she moved close to the bed. Her body was equally aroused and craved his attention. All in due time, she figured. Following her whim, she straddled him, but lowered her body onto his stomach.

His arousal was moist with anticipation. She looked forward to sheathing his raw desire. Her fingers nestled along the curled hairs of his chest, down past his stomach, disappearing into a thick mass of unruliness.

"You're going to pay for this." He writhed between her legs, his teeth clenched, fingers curled and uncurled.

She leaned down and kissed him, savoring the feel of his lips between hers before succumbing to the erotic dance with his tongue. "You'll pay soon enough."

In one fluid move, she replaced her lips against his mouth with the tips of her breasts. His neck arched and his mouth opened, in anticipation of her nipple. She balanced herself, lightly brushing his lips until his tongue flicked a blazing path around her nipple before fastening on with a strong suction.

Her eyes squeezed shut and it was her turn to suck air between her teeth. What Jaden awakened had been buried deep under layers of cynicism and behind heavy drapes of insecurities. The powerful swell of desire started like a soft rolling wind rustling and nudging her sexual appetite.

Rubbing against the full length of his body, feeling his arousal next to her skin, sliding along the length of his thighs—she escalated the forces of her desire into a raging gale with an overpowering strength that surged to a climactic peak.

"You can't be so cruel," Jaden complained. The powerful long muscles in his thighs contracted. His toes cracked as he flexed them.

Denise couldn't take credit for being merciful. She slipped on the condom, looking forward to the immediate future.

She untied him.

They panted, exuding a calm that warned of a stormy union soon to come.

Her hands encircled him as she lowered herself onto him, taking him fully into her. She was sure that he would see her heart pounding against her ribs. The hunger between her legs sought its satisfaction as she rocked against Jaden. Their rhythm resembled dancers partnered in a sensual tango of fluidity and grace with their hips locked into place.

And there she stayed until Jaden signaled his readiness by squeezing her hips. She willingly followed him, holding on to his shoulders as the orgasmic waves rolled and pounded over them, like they were powerless survivors against an incoming tide.

Denise hung on for dear life. The power of speech had been seized. Even if she could open her eyes, she doubted that she'd be able to see. The roar of their passion defeated her. Only her sense of touch remained, enjoying the play of his muscles under her fingers.

"Please don't let this be over anytime soon," her mind cried out.

Chapter 6

Jaden entered his parents' home, a cozy ranch-style bungalow where they hadn't needed to handle stairs. They had recently moved into a senior living facility that looked like paradise. A large flowing fountain greeted residents and visitors at the main entrance. A huge community center took center stage, surrounded by condos, bungalows, townhomes and duplexes.

His mother had pushed for the change of residence. His father's health had always been rocky. She didn't want to deal with a large house and his health emergencies.

"Jaden, good to see you. I had my doubts that you'd show up."

"Why?" He kissed her cheek and entered their bungalow, inhaling the wonderful scent of home-cooked food.

"Calvin said that you probably wouldn't be here. He mentioned a new friend named Denise." His mother wiggled her eyebrows. Her shocking white hair was pulled into a ponytail. "How come I haven't met with your young lady?"

Jaden took a deep breath for patience at hearing of his brother's involvement. "Calvin doesn't know what he's talking about. She's just a friend." He headed to the family room, which he knew his father had staked out as his haven. Right about now he wanted in.

He opened the door and stepped in but stopped short. Calvin and his father were playing chess. They both looked up at him. Jaden wanted to back out but stood his ground. Maybe he could get through the evening without a battle that had no purpose.

"Hi, Pop." He patted his father's shoulder, noticing how frail his body felt under his fingers. "Hey, Calvin." He nodded to his brother, immediately noticing the glass of amber liquid. His father always kept a bottle of Scotch, although he had long since stopped drinking because of his prescription drugs.

"Is dinner ready?" His father peered over his reading glasses at him.

"I'll go check." Jaden sought to escape, feeling like an intruder.

"Need any help?" he asked his mother as he entered the kitchen.

"Did they kick you out?" His mother patted his arm. "Calvin and your father haven't had a special time like that in a while. It pleases my heart to see them together." She handed him a stack of plates. "Set the table, please."

Preparing the table for their dinner allowed him the time to chat with his mother. She always liked to hear how the houses had been renovated. Occasionally he took her to the sites to see his projects.

"Looks like we're ready to eat. Get your father and brother."

Jaden headed back to the family room. He opened the door in time to see Calvin take a wad of cash from his father. They both started when Jaden announced, "Dinner is ready." He glared at his father, who defiantly glared back. He didn't bother to look at Calvin, knowing there would be no sign of remorse.

Dinner proceeded smoothly, or as smoothly as possible. Jaden kept his conversation on the weather, his projects and the change in the neighborhood. His mother chatted about her herb garden, her neighbors and his projects. His father barely spoke and when he did his attention was on Calvin.

"I'll help with dessert, Mom." Calvin followed his mother into the kitchen.

Jaden couldn't take it any longer. He leaned over to his father. "Why would you give him any alcohol? You're not helping the problem."

"He is my son. As long as I have breath in my body, I will help him. It was just a celebratory drink. He's going to stay here and get better."

Jaden straightened up when his mother returned. She looked at him and then at his father. Her mouth pursed but she said nothing.

Calvin carried a yellow cake with icing drizzled over the top. The scent of lemon hinted at the flavor.

"Mom, I'm going to move in for a little while." Calvin grinned but was too old and haggard to pull off the little-boy routine.

"Oh." His mother's reaction alerted Jaden that she hadn't been consulted on this latest development.

"I thought there were rules about who could live in a senior living facility." Jaden couldn't help but push his point.

"That's outrageous that they can tell me who I can have in my house," his father blustered. "Your mother should've never forced me to come live in this prison."

"He can stay up to two weeks." His mother

looked over her glasses at her younger son. "Then he'll have to go."

"That's enough time, right, son?" His father smiled at Calvin.

Calvin didn't share their enthusiasm. Jaden surmised the reason. He didn't have a job and, in his condition, he would have a hard time holding one down.

"It's not a good idea to test the rules. You just arrived," Jaden advised.

"We wouldn't have to step in if you would've helped," his father replied.

His mother's downward gaze was fastened on her slice of cake; Jaden wondered if she agreed with her husband's summation.

"I wouldn't want to impose on Jaden, considering he's got a girlfriend who has practically made his house her second home," Calvin said.

"This is the same young lady who hasn't been introduced to us." His mother's disapproval landed squarely at Jaden's feet.

"I don't have a problem with Calvin staying with me, but only under certain conditions."

"There aren't conditions when you are dealing with family," his father declared. "Your grandparents didn't raise our family with conditions. You didn't go outside the unit for help."

"Those were different times," Jaden replied. "I'm not going to change my mind. He can only live with me when he has his life under control."

"And you're a role model of structure and order." Calvin disappeared into the family room and brought out a glassful of Scotch. "I figured we should have a toast to you."

"Oh, dear," his mother exclaimed and immediately started clearing the table.

Jaden ate his cake.

"I want to toast Jaden on his successful millionaire lifestyle. He's got a babe magnet of a car. And when Charlene and her son got to be too much for him, he went and got a younger model."

"Bring that girl to this house." His father glowered at Jaden. "I'll decide whether she's a good girl or not."

"I had no intention of hiding Denise. We are still getting to know each other and we are taking things slowly. I respect that." Jaden pushed away from the table. "Looks like it's time for me to get going." He headed for the kitchen. "Thanks for dinner, Mom." He kissed her cheek.

"Please don't go. You know we love you."

Jaden nodded. All this dysfunction in the name of love. He looked forward to going home and having a quiet evening. Regardless of the pressure that his father applied, he was not going to let Calvin into his house unless he was in a program.

He headed home, thinking about Denise. How could he possibly bring her into his chaotic family situation? His father's attitude was unpredictable. His mother, with her blind optimism, acted as if she were stuck in the 1950s, and his brother could be counted on to be rude and boorish. No way was Denise walking into that mess.

When he got home, he unwound with a couple of laps in the pool. By the time he was done, he badly wanted to talk to Denise. When he finally settled into bed, he dialed her number. Hearing the sound of her voice and flirting outrageously with her ranked at the top of his list of great ways to fall asleep. The phone rang until the voice mail kicked in. He left a message, more than a little disappointed that he only had memories to keep him until he fell asleep.

Denise sat in her government-provided SUV waiting for the shift change to be complete. Her least favorite part of her job was playing stakeout in the late hours of the evening on a street where she'd never walk during daylight. However, production reports for this unit raised warning signals. Normally she'd delegate this to one of her senior supervisors, but since she didn't know how deep this problem was, she'd opted to run her informal investigation.

The new shift showed up at the work site. The supervisors conferred, transferring information to their respective clipboards. The crew going back to the maintenance yard loaded up their trucks and vans and headed out. Denise slid down in the seat until they passed.

Now her vigilance counted. She pulled an apple out of her paper bag and munched as the new crew pulled out their equipment to do their work. So far, everything looked normal. Maybe the reports were false or involved a different crew. She was wasting a perfectly good night's sleep for this.

She had eaten the apple down to the core before something caught her attention. A van filled with four employees departed from the site. They'd barely arrived on the site, so it couldn't be their break time. Denise sat up, fully alert.

She started the car, deciding to follow them. Now, this was fun. The van ahead turned down several side streets, then pulled up in front of a liquor store. Denise pulled into an empty parking space and watched. She couldn't believe the employees' brazen act, walking out with a case of beer. They loaded up the van and returned to the site.

She waited until they'd parked the van and unloaded their treat before she strolled into their presence.

"Gentlemen, may I have your attention." She pointed at her badge. "No, don't bother, I've already seen what I needed to see." She raised her hand to halt the stream of defenses thrown at her. "A new crew is on its way. You can pack up and leave. H.R. will be in touch with the necessary procedures."

She walked back to her SUV and pulled off. Her undercover tactics wouldn't endear her to the field crews. But she also had to show them that she was capable of hard business decisions. To allow a rogue crew to do whatever it wanted was inviting problems.

The payback for her trouble was lots of paperwork to be filed. She went to her office, opting to begin the process now rather than wait until the morning.

With the soft rays of morning breaking the horizon, Denise filled out the lengthy packet of paperwork, her cup of hot coffee near at hand. Whenever her thoughts deviated from the task, she took a long sip from her mug. This wasn't the time to think about Jaden.

Her admission about her problem hadn't brought a reaction. She didn't know whether that was bad or not. Although she was grateful that he didn't condemn her, she suspected that it didn't warm his heart. But he had been so sweet while he helped her move.

Maybe there was hope. He had said he appreciated her honesty.

A week later, Denise spent another long evening at her desk. Again, she waved at the cleaning service as they began their duties. She turned her attention to the computer monitor, studying the spreadsheet she'd created.

She could take this stuff home and work on it; however, her mood wasn't terribly upbeat. She and Jaden had played telephone tag. The longer the gap grew from the time she had spoken to Jaden, the worse her temper got.

The good news was that he had mentioned how much he missed her. All she could settle on was listening to his voice on the answering machine.

Her computer beeped, alerting her that there was a new e-mail message.

She clicked on the screen.

Hey, Soror,
Have you heard the latest? Can't seem to get in touch with you. Sara set a date for the wedding. Finally. In three months. Can you believe that she's doing it so quickly? Probably scared that she can't pin down Jackson. LOL. Buzz me.
Sisterly,
Athena.

Denise clapped her hands and pumped her fist in the air. This was absolutely fantastic news. Sara would be the first in their inner circle to be married.

Each soror had talked about her fantasy wedding. But Denise had problems imagining anything beyond a small, family affair in the backyard. Why have anything lavish when you stood a great chance of ending in divorce court?

Sara had found her soul mate. Denise didn't think that she'd be that lucky. She replied to Athena's e-mail.

I'm still working. Ready to fall over. Thanks for the good news. So we're looking at a wedding in the dead of summer. Hope it's not outdoors.
D—

Denise finished up her work and shut down her computer. She stretched her neck and shoulders. Right now she would pay a hefty price for a massage. She packed her briefcase and headed home. The best she could do would be to turn her showerhead to pulse and let the water stream beat down on her back.

When she arrived home, there was a note pinned to her door. She looked around to see if anyone was waiting for her to open the door. Rather than hang outside reading the note, she opened the door quickly and closed it behind her, turning the locks.

The message brought a huge grin. She called Jaden's cell phone. "Stop scaring me. Come in." When she heard his footsteps, she looked through the peephole then opened the door.

He greeted her with a wet, sloppy kiss. "I missed you. It's been a crazy week. I can't believe that we haven't had a chance to see each other."

"I kind of thought that you didn't want to see me anymore."

"Stop thinking like that." He kissed her again. She loved the strength of his arms around her. He made her feel wanted and desirable. She answered his kiss with equal passion.

She kicked off her shoes and headed for the kitchen. "Want a turkey sandwich?"

"Sure."

As she gathered the ingredients for their sandwiches, she updated him on Sara's new turn of events. He peppered the conversation with lots of questions about how they had gotten Jackson back into Sara's life and the romantic details.

"Didn't realize that you were so romantic. You love a happy ending," Jaden said, taking a bag of barbecue potato chips from her.

"Romance has its plus side." She grinned, loving

the way he smiled at her. "I'd say we're having a pretty good one." She pushed it into the center of the conversation without a backup plan in case he pushed it right off to the side.

He sighed with a satisfied grin on his face. She couldn't tell whether he was happy from eating the barbecue chips or because he agreed with her. When he didn't open his eyes, she tossed a crust of bread at him, hitting him squarely on the forehead.

"What?"

"When you describe us to people, what do you say?"

He looked up at the ceiling, making popping sounds with his lips. Then he arched an eyebrow. "You know what, I don't talk about us." He raised his hand when she shot forward. "And I don't talk about us because I'm a very private person."

"That may be so, but there has to be someone you confide in. I have my sorority sisters and I'm closer to them than my real sister." She wrinkled her nose.

"Guess I can say the same about me and my brother. I do have a good buddy from college. His name is Leonard. I would probably confide in him."

"But you didn't." Denise noted the nervous tapping of his foot. She wanted to know the whys of Jaden's thought process. His answers would reveal a lot, but if he chose not to answer, she'd know more than she wanted to.

"Like I said, I keep things close." He balled his hand into a fist and pounded his chest. "Leonard has a wife on bed rest. At this point, I listen to him."

Denise stopped probing. As close as they were, she realized there was a lot that she didn't know. Did Jaden talk on the phone about the latest basketball scores with his friends? Did he volunteer at a homeless shelter? Or did he suffer from road rage? Did he double dip his chips?

"I'm not that complicated. You're making things bigger than they have to be. Remember, I'm your friendly neighborhood contractor."

"What about me? What would you like to know?" She propped her chin on her hand and waited.

"I think anything that I want to know, I can get from your sorority sisters."

"Oh, really? They are sworn to secrecy."

He pulled out his cell phone and dialed.

"Who are you calling?"

"Athena."

Denise sprang out of the chair and circled the table. But Jaden was too fast and jumped up from the table, heading down the hall toward the doors leading to the deck.

"Athena. Hi, it's Jaden. Yeah, how are you?" He restrained Denise on a nearby sofa with one arm across her chest. "We have this bet going on. What was Denise's weight in college?"

Denise laughed and screamed at the same time. "Don't tell him. Don't!"

Jaden grinned at her and snapped the phone closed. Then he walked past her and headed into the bathroom. "Are you coming?"

Denise debated calling Athena to find out what she'd told Jaden. But her line sister wouldn't betray her, or would she? And of all things to ask—her weight.

"I can hear you thinking from up here."

"Good, then you know what I'm thinking right now." She smiled. She hoped this man would be around for a long time.

"Uh-oh."

She listened to Jaden's heavy footsteps coming down the steps. She didn't move from the sofa. Instead he moved into her view with a boyish grin.

"Don't even think about it." Denise squirmed away from his attempt to kiss her.

"It's going to be a cold night, huh?"

"I should think so."

"What if I told you that she didn't tell me anything. Call her."

She shifted her position.

"Or you could just trust me that I didn't hear anything."

Denise looked at the phone on the side table, then up at him. "I'll trust you."

"Your mouth is saying one thing, but those eyes…" He shook his head. "I feel there's more."

"I want to meet Leonard. I want you to bring me into your world."

Jaden showed his surprise. A small frown played with his furrowed brow. He still hadn't met her gaze. Unease churned her stomach. His hesitation alarmed her.

"How about meeting my parents?"

"I'm judging that you're doing this under duress. I don't want it to be that way." Denise backed off.

"Will you come to bed?"

Denise looked at her watch. "Good grief, I have an early day ahead of me." She walked up the stairs with Jaden. "I'm not sleeping with you."

"The only reason that I'm hesitant is because of the problems with my brother and its effect on my family. I don't want to bring you into something tense."

Denise heard beyond the words he uttered. Her family situation wasn't ideal, either. And she didn't entertain the notion of bringing Jaden into that mess. Nevertheless, getting the approval of a significant family member was part of elevating a relationship.

She observed the ease with which he moved around her room. They enjoyed each other physically, but there was more to them than the orgasmic pleasure they got from each other.

"I look forward to meeting your parents." She slipped under the covers and waited for him to join her.

He gently drew her to him and she snuggled against the warmth of his body. Her muscles relaxed as her mind drifted lazily, on the verge of falling asleep. She felt his tender kiss on her forehead. She closed her eyes and burrowed deeper into his embrace. "You're still not getting any."

Denise would rather be anywhere than sitting in a restaurant with her sister. "Aren't you going to order something?"

"I told you that I don't like Thai. Yet you insist on having me meet you in these places." Thea sniffed, visibly distressed by her surroundings.

"Then you should've picked the place."

"I didn't want to inconvenience you."

"Too late."

Thea glared. "It's Mom and Dad's anniversary. We need to plan a party."

"It's not a milestone. There's no need to go over the top." Denise looked down the pages of the oversize menu. Photos of the various dishes added to her longing for Thai. It was a toss-up between beef kee mao and pad thai. Normally her sorors would share with her, but she knew better than to make such a suggestion to Thea.

"I think otherwise." Thea pulled out a colorful brochure and set it down on the table with a punctuated thud. "This place would be fabulous. They can have a seated dinner, live music and a good number of guests. The best thing is that the facility has a screen and projector. We could show pictures of them through their marriage." Thea beamed over the disclosure of her ideas.

Instead of immediately responding, Denise placed her order. She ordered the pad thai for lunch and the kee mao for dinner. With the generous portions, she'd have leftovers for the remainder of the week.

"Let me handle the agenda and you can handle the guest lists," Thea said. "Your busy schedule shouldn't be affected."

"Thea, you have no idea what my day is like."

"And whose fault is that?" Thea grimaced when the food arrived. She placed a delicate finger under her nose. "We barely see you. When we do, you're at war with all of us. We are worried about you. Is everything okay? That guy at the casino party. Is that the latest guy in your life? He looks a little regular." She stopped when Denise pointed her fork at her. "If that's what makes you happy," Thea continued, "go ahead."

Denise clamped her mouth shut. Almost. She had

almost fallen into the trap. Thea was trying to bait her and did this intricate dance to find out about Jaden. Instead of answering Thea's list of questions, Denise dug into her food, enjoying the sweet, nutty flavor of the pad thai.

"You're being stubborn, you know. Fine. Don't talk about your new man. The guest list?"

"I'll work on the list. Get me the names and addresses."

"I also have another idea. I want Dad and his brother to make up. I want to invite him to the anniversary as a surprise."

Denise looked up sharply. "Does Mom know about this?"

Thea shook her head. "Could you hurry up and eat that stuff? You do realize that shrimp are scavengers."

"I'm not sure the reunion schtick is a good idea. Maybe Dad has a good reason for not dealing with Floyd anymore."

"I think it's about time that we bring Uncle Floyd in from exile. I also want Nate to fly in from whatever remote place he's in, so all of us, the siblings, will be here." Thea leaned closer. "Please, Denise, don't make things difficult. I want us to be the way we used to be. One big happy family." She reached over and held Denise's hand.

"Everything else I can live with," Denise replied.

"But Floyd doesn't need to be invited." Then she looked at her sister's stubborn countenance. "Wait a minute. Have you been in touch with him?"

Thea didn't meet her scrutiny, although she shook her head.

"I don't believe you. Tell me you didn't contact him."

"Why? Because you say so?" Thea gathered up her pocketbook. "You're not in control of this." She rose from her seat. "Let's meet again. Next time, we will meet at the Tea Palace."

"When is Dad returning? It's this Sunday, isn't it?"

Thea stopped her departure abruptly. "Don't you dare."

"I'll be over on Sunday."

Thea headed back to the table; then, just before she started talking, she stopped and walked away.

Denise signaled the waitress and asked for her bill. In a matter of minutes, she had exited the restaurant with her meal in hand. Before, she had been mildly irritated by Thea and her grand plans, but now she was beyond furious with her sister's latest strategy.

Floyd, and he would never be her uncle, had no business near her parents. If she never saw him again she wouldn't be sad. So many years had gone by but she'd never forget.

* * *

Jaden arrived back at his home since he didn't have any meetings that morning. He'd work out before meeting with his project manager for a final status report on Denise's property. Even though he benefited greatly from this project, he always got a sense of pride for completing one.

His good mood evaporated in a whiff. Calvin was prone against his front door. The smell of sweat, alcohol and body odor surrounded him in an invisible cloud. Jaden stood over his brother's still body, listening to the soft buzz of his snore.

He glanced around, wondering if any of his neighbors had caught an eyeful. He stooped over Calvin, nudging him with the back of his hand. When his brother didn't budge, he pushed against him much harder.

"Wh-what! Get..." Calvin's hand flailed in the air. Jaden tilted his head back to avoid getting hit in the nose.

"Look, get up, Calvin." He leaned in close to Calvin's ear. "Move it!"

Calvin opened his eyes and yawned, his breath filled with alcohol vapors. "You are loud and obnoxious." He rolled onto his side and began to make himself comfortable.

"Oh, no, you don't. Sleeping time on the front

porch is over. I will help you up." Jaden placed his forearms under his brother's armpits. "Come on, move it."

His brother didn't cooperate until Jaden shook his shoulder with great force. As Calvin uttered a string of curses, Jaden shifted his weight and used his leg muscles to heft Calvin from a prone position to stand relatively upright. His legs buckled and couldn't seem to gain stability.

"Calvin, you've got to help." Jaden stumbled with his brother's weight into the house. He couldn't close the door without losing his burden. They barely made it to the sofa before he fell, with Calvin pinning him.

At this point, he didn't care to be considerate and pushed Calvin off his body. Now wasn't the time to lecture him. He closed the front door. Disgusted, he went up to his room and prepared for bed.

Initially he'd planned to come home, call Denise and flirt outrageously over the phone. He would declare to no one that he was smitten. Yet he couldn't stop thinking about her. And when he was in her presence, he wanted to touch her, to permanently etch into his memory the softness of her skin, the gentle, floral scent of her cologne or the sweet taste of her lips.

A huge risk loomed ahead at the thought of bringing her into his hectic family life. He feared that whatever feelings she would have for him may turn to revulsion with the ugliness of alcoholism and its side effects on his family.

He wanted Denise to believe that she was more to him than a fling. Short of telling her that he loved her, he had to rely on certain sincere acts. Saying "I love you" was out of the question. People changed when love entered the game.

Jaden drifted to sleep with the image of Denise smiling up at him in her sexy red nightie.

"Jaden!"

Jaden awoke with a start. His eyes opened, staring at his wall. The room was dark. He blinked, wondering if it was morning.

He sensed someone in the room with him. He turned over, scanning the room since his eyes had gotten used to the darkness.

"Jaden."

"Calvin?" He saw a dark, hulking shape near his door, close to the floor. "Calvin?" He rose from the bed and hurried over to his brother who was taken over by dry heaves. Jaden didn't know what to do, how to give comfort or take away the obvious pain.

Instead of listening to his brother's moans through the night, he dialed the emergency number. He ran down to unlock the door and leave it slightly ajar. Then he ran back to his brother, who was now facedown, clammy and listless. Jaden stayed at his side, wiping the moisture from his face with the comforter he'd pulled off his bed.

Finally he heard the siren approach. After the sound of doors slamming, someone knocked at the front door.

"Come in, I'm up here. Come up the stairs." He leaned out into the hallway, hoping to see them in a matter of seconds.

On cue, a paramedic appeared and then another. They promptly identified themselves, then turned their attention to Calvin.

"He's been drinking. I don't know how much or how long ago. I left him on the sofa downstairs. He looked as if he was asleep. I came up here and crashed. Then he woke me up, calling my name."

"So he was conscious?" The first paramedic, who looked like he'd barely passed his teens, was checking his pulse.

"Yes. Then he started moaning and passed out." He looked down at the comforter in his hand. "I had to move him a little so I could get the comforter around him."

Calvin stirred. His eyes opened but he had difficulty focusing. His lips moved but no sound emerged. The muscles in his neck strained. Jaden realized that he was trying to raise his head, but his body was too weak to comply.

"We've got to get him to the hospital."

"What do you think it is?"

"You'll have to wait for the doctors to check him out."

Jaden followed the team as they rolled Calvin to the top of the stairs on a stretcher and then lifted him down the stairs. Jaden wanted to help, but they efficiently managed without him.

He followed, taking the time to alert his parents.

Jaden sat with his parents in the hospital cafeteria. They each had a cup of coffee in front of them. The breakfast hours were nearly over and the facility emptied. The doctor's prognosis was hard news to bear.

"We need to get a second opinion." His father laid his palms flat against the table, his fingers splayed across the surface.

"Dad, there is no need for a second opinion. Calvin has alcohol poisoning and is lucky that he's not dead. We know he has a problem. And on a good, coherent day, Calvin knows he has a problem. You are the only one who seems to look the other way. That's not helping him."

"Don't disrespect your father. Calvin needs loving care. This is why I insist he come home."

"You are not a professional, Mom. No offense."

"Well, offense is taken because I'm his mother. I

know Calvin. We don't need an overpriced, over-educated professional to dig into his head and put all kinds of nonsense in there."

His father rose and waited for his mother to stand next to him. "He'll stay here for a few days. Then he comes home. We're going to see him now."

Jaden took the emphasis of "we" to mean that he was excluded.

"This might not have happened if he'd been staying with you," his father accused.

Jaden kept his hands around the small coffee cup to keep warm against the frigid anger of his father. He knew that his parents hurt and he tried to keep that in mind as they looked for any place or person to hang their blame.

He waited half an hour before heading up to see his brother. As he walked the corridors, inhaling the strong, pungent aroma of disinfectant and human misery, fear matched his strides even as he walked more slowly when he entered the unit.

As big brother, the role of protector came naturally. Through high school and college, he responded to all of Calvin's requests for help, no matter how insignificant. As they got older, the bond that he thought would tighten as they matured instead grew brittle.

Seeing the aftereffects of too much booze was a megaphone for how fragile life was. Jaden looked down at the figure bloated with shadows of his hardship. He gritted his teeth to hold on to his emotions, on the brink of unraveling. He couldn't let his brother slip away any further.

"I'm a mess, aren't I?" His brother's voice sounded like sandpaper.

Jaden wiggled his eyebrows. His throat felt constricted.

"I pretended to be out of it when Mom and Dad were here." Calvin closed his eyes. "I'll do better when I'm out of here." He pulled at his gown.

Jaden shook his head. "No, I don't think you can. And this is too hard on them. I have to step up for you and their sake."

"What?"

"When you leave here, you're going straight into a rehab facility. You don't have to worry about the expenses. We'll find the right one for you."

"I could be out as early as tomorrow."

"We'll manage."

"No. I need time to think about this. Dad is going to help me."

"He can't." Jaden took a deep breath to lower his voice. "Dad has his own medical issues to deal with. He's a handful for Mom. What do you think you'll do to her or them?"

"I don't have to stay with them. I can stay with you."

Jaden hated to see his brother's increased agitation as his hands feverishly pulled at the covers. His forehead had a thin sheen of sweat.

Calvin put a hand over his face. He didn't say anything for several long seconds. "I don't believe this is happening."

"Trust me." Jaden's entire body tensed for his brother's response.

"Okay, I'll go."

Jaden clapped his hands. Overwhelming emotion swelled in his chest. He pressed his clasped hands to his lips. Gratitude poured out of him. Slowly a part of him that he didn't even know he'd closed off relaxed, allowing in a ray of hope.

He left the room shortly after, heading to the nurses' station to leave a message for the doctor. He'd need the doctor to give him twenty-four hours to find a facility. Once he had Calvin registered, then he'd tell his parents.

Jaden returned home to shower and take on his new project of finding a drug rehabilitation center. He called his doctor for referrals, used various search engines on the Internet and asked a few of his friends who may have had to use such a facility.

After making a short list and starting the interview process, he concluded that it was sad that so many treatment centers were needed in the first place.

Finally he settled on one in Florida that catered to clients with deep pocketbooks. Maybe guilt led his decision, but he settled all the details over the phone.

Jaden decided to fly with him to the center, which arranged to have one of its attendants meet them at the airport when they arrived.

With the better part of the day complete, he rescheduled his upcoming meetings. He wondered if Denise was still in her office. That wasn't the real issue. How much to tell her? What to tell her? These questions rumbled around in his mind looking for the right answers. She might not hold it against him, but her family would be mortified. His parents would have had a fit if he'd brought home a woman who had a close relative who was an addict.

Denise answered his call on the first ring. "Hey, I was thinking about you."

"Same here. Busy?"

"Same thing, different day. How about yourself? You sound kind of tired."

"Dealing with the family. As a matter of fact, I'm heading out of town tomorrow."

"I don't have any events where you can pop up and surprise me." Her voice was warm and inviting.

Jaden shared a laugh. "I'll be gone for a couple of days. I'll call you."

"Sure."

He detected a slight hesitation.

Jaden hung up, not pleased with the way he'd handled the call. Now she was probably suspicious and angry when there was no cause for her concern. He'd handle one crisis at a time. Right now he had to focus on Calvin.

When he got back, he'd turn his attention to Denise. It was a promise.

Chapter 7

"It's raining." Denise complained to no avail. Athena and Asia wore one of their few identical outfits, a slate-gray exercise suit. Denise dragged herself around the house as she located socks and then tennis shoes.

"The time doesn't start until we're at the track. You can stop dawdling." Athena sat on the edge of the chair's arm in Denise's bedroom. Denise made quite a sexy picture in her powder-blue-and-white sweatsuit.

Denise looked at her reflection, swearing that her hips had doubled since the last time she weighed. Not being able to fit into her favorite pair of jeans provided enough motivation to join Asia and Athena's training workout. However, her plan was to stay safely in a gym riding a bike while chatting about the latest celebrity gossip. Instead, her girls had her running outside.

They got in the car and drove to a nearby college stadium and track. "Are you going to get out of the car today?" Asia asked.

"I'm not really feeling like it today. I change my mind."

"Oh, no, you don't. You get mopey every time that Jaden doesn't call you or goes away."

"I do not. No man is going to control my emotions like that."

"When love is involved you don't have any control over your emotions," Athena chimed in.

"Um…and what would you know about that?" Denise turned to glare at Athena in the backseat. Her soror had her pick of the hunky college guys. Now she barely dated. The second that a guy got too attached or clingy, they all knew that he was a goner.

"I'm getting out to run. It's a light rain." Asia stepped out wearing her poncho. She pulled up the hood and headed to the track.

"How could you have a sister who doesn't care about her hair? What grown African-American woman would allow her hair to get wet in a downpour?"

"Her new braids will survive it. And Asia has become the health nut, way more than I ever did. Everything is organic and vegetarian. She said that she's going natural. And she doesn't even shave her legs anymore."

"Sounds like she needs an intervention. I hope she's shaving her underarms."

"Can't promise."

"I hope she'll find a man who can see past the 'natural' bushiness to appreciate her inner beauty."

There was dead silence, then both women laughed heartily.

"Let's go before she makes us do extra laps."

"I'm only running the stadium stairs once." Denise looked up at the daunting height of the stadium seats rising sharply into the air. Going up the narrow steps was difficult, but coming down was worse. She felt like a mountain goat without the sure-footedness.

The three women jogged around the track. Conversation peaked and died as they passed the one-mile mark for the third time. No one else joined them as they progressed through the exercise regimen.

"Time for the stairs." Asia jogged off toward the stadium, leaving her two running partners.

Denise felt as if a lung would pop out. She had no energy to get up the stairs. While Asia ran ahead, she leaned over and placed her hands on her knees to catch her breath.

"What a bunch of freakin' losers!"

Denise shot upright. Her face broke into a wide grin. "Naomi!" She ran to her soror, who was also in her running gear but without a poncho.

"Let's walk up halfway so I can talk to you," Denise bargained.

"Sure." Naomi turned to Athena, who had waited for Denise. "What's up, girl?"

"I've been cool. Good to see you."

Denise saved her breath to conquer the stairs. Even though she walked up the steps, which was the only way for her to surmount them, she would come down much more quickly.

At the top they each took a seat. The rain had stopped. Up there the wind blew away the humidity. Denise peeled off her poncho, followed by her line sisters. The world below appeared so small.

"I've missed everyone."

"We've missed you, too," Asia said.

"Have you heard that Sara has set the date?" Denise filled her in.

"No, I missed that. Are we going to do something?" Naomi rubbed her ankle.

"What are your schedules like? You know she'll try to do things on her own," Athena remarked.

"I'm free this weekend if she wants to go look at stuff."

"Where's your man?" Naomi asked.

"Please don't ask her anything about Jaden or she'll go into her funk." Asia rolled her eyes.

Denise took the teasing as a sign for her to begin to descend the steps. She didn't respond as they continued to talk about her and Jaden.

Sara had found her true love and her life had been transformed. Denise wasn't looking for transformation or a makeover. She wasn't even looking for love, or was she prepared to admit to finding it.

Naomi placed her arm around her shoulder. "Are you cool on all fronts?"

Denise wasn't sure what she referred to. But one look at her face and the sweet concern that was shared between friends and she understood. "I'm fine. Look at me, don't I look fine?" Her defenses were too fragile to withstand Naomi's kindness. It took sheer willpower to keep her tears hidden. She was determined to work on this problem herself. She'd already dragged everyone into her life by borrowing money. This stuff she'd keep to herself.

"The girls filled me in on what happened at the fund-raiser."

"Good grief. You all are a trip. You act as if you live these perfect lives." Her agitation brought silence over the group. She kept her eyes focused forward. She was embarrassed and couldn't handle looking at them and seeing pity, accusation and maybe anger.

"We don't hide things from each other," Asia said.

"But you don't have to keep waving a flag like it's something that defines me."

"You take ownership of your vice and then you can control it." Naomi took her hand.

Denise snatched her hand back. She bit back the caustic remark that she wanted to fling back at Naomi for turning the spotlight on her problem.

"Now isn't the time." Athena patted her knee. "Has anyone spoken to Sara lately?"

"Let's call her." Asia pulled out her cell phone. They leaned against the cars, cooling down before heading back home.

Denise listened to Asia pull the necessary information out of Sara. She was going to look at two venues.

"I'm in. Anyone else?" Athena looked pointedly at Naomi.

"I can make it," Naomi answered, but her face revealed that she wasn't sure if she would.

"Let's meet over at Sara's by one o'clock."

They agreed before departing from the parking lot.

Denise took her shower before checking her messages. She listened to the answering machine, waiting for his voice. Nothing. He hadn't called her. When the phone did ring, she grabbed it, greeting the caller with a natural exuberance.

"Denise, I've been trying to reach you. I have the guest list, but we need to discuss a few things. Meet me at Mom and Dad's tomorrow. Five o'clock works for me."

"Fine, Thea." Denise automatically wanted to be difficult and disagreeable, but common sense prevailed. "I'll meet you there."

"Remember that we're not going to talk about Uncle Floyd."

"Bye." Denise hung up. She wasn't budging from her position that Floyd wasn't coming to her parents' anniversary celebration.

She finished dressing and headed over to Sara's. As she pulled into a parking spot, Asia arrived. Athena followed, with Naomi sitting beside her. Right on time, Sara exited from her house and walked over to their cars.

"Are we taking one car?" Sara asked.

"Denise's is the one with the most room."

"Her SUV will work but she's not the best driver." Athena entered Denise's car to sit in the backseat. "I don't need to see the moment of impact."

"Shut up. Get in or get left." Denise revved the engine, enjoying seeing them scramble into her car.

The first destination was two florists that specialized in weddings. Their group descended on each business in noisy fashion, blowing past their affected, sophisticated atmosphere. No one could contain their good mood.

"I'm not trying to spend a gazillion dollars." Sara's frowned deepened as her finger trailed down the prices in the catalog.

"Price shouldn't matter at a special time like this," the saleswoman said. "You want to look sophisticated and romantic. This is the display that you could have, and then you could go with this beautiful bouquet with crisp white roses in the center, and blossoms on the outer edge that have a soft, barely visible touch of red on the tips of the petals."

"Sounds fantastic." Athena held up the sample, pretending that she was a bride.

"Here, let me see." Asia took the bouquet from her sister.

"What do you think?" Sara turned to ask Denise.

Denise nodded. Sara could trust her to be truthful and understand her tastes. The saleslady may have been a snob but she knew her business. Denise had to agree that the flowers would help transform the wedding. They told the florist they'd be back once they had picked the reception site.

Most of the other details were handled, except for

the place for the reception. They drove to various hotels and facilities advertising for such events. Some had an annoying cheesiness that made her do a U-turn in the parking lot and head for the next one on the list.

"After this, I want to stop for food. I'm starving," Naomi declared with major irritation.

Denise looked over at Sara. "Do you have to get back?"

"No. Jackson is busy picking out tuxes. Preparing a wedding, especially on short notice, is tiring."

"Stop trying to do everything. We're here to help you. And you know that I have your back." Denise always had to prod Sara to give up control. But she didn't want to see her friend wear herself to the point of exhaustion when they were all here to help. "I know that you'll have a beautiful, memorable wedding."

"Hear! Hear!" The chorus of agreement filled the car as they all yelled.

"Okay, where is this place? I feel like we've driven into Canada by now." Naomi groaned in the back. "My legs are almost in my chest."

Sara pulled out the directions. "From what I've read, we should be there in another fifteen minutes." She looked out the window. "We certainly are in farm country."

"Who recommended this place?"

"One of Jackson's business partners told him about it."

"Oh, I think we're here." Denise turned down an unpaved road that cut through two large fields. The car crunched against the gravel following the tracks. Then it veered sharply to the right through a wide gateway. The rough gravel gave way to a stone driveway with a large, country manor–style house at its end.

"I feel like we're on a British country estate." Sara opened her window and peered outside.

"Stop the car." Athena tapped the back of Denise's seat.

Denise didn't argue, since she wanted the chance to get out and explore. The parking lot had a few cars, but it didn't alter the charming surroundings.

Vines partially covered the front face of the building, which must have been someone's home. The historic architecture modeled simple lines, balanced and efficient, but there was a classical elegance that spoke of an earlier period.

"When I grow up I want a house just like this." Naomi stretched out her arms and spun around. "Now all I need is the man to go with the house."

"Let's go in. We've got to find someone named Lucinda Childress." Sara walked in with her nose in the air. That was all the twins needed, as they followed with their noses in the air. Naomi winked at Denise, hooked arms and they strode in, arm in arm.

"How may we help you?" A woman who looked as if she could have grown up in the house stood in front of them in an uncomfortable-looking suit. She didn't offer her hand, but that didn't stop Sara from shooting her hand out to the woman.

Denise wanted to giggle. This woman had better not be the sales rep. While they waited for Lucinda to come talk to them, Denise headed down a hallway to view several framed black-and-white photographs hanging on the wall. According to the small gold-plated tag at the bottom of the photos, this was a pictorial history of the city's Underground Railroad leaders and the homes involved in the movement.

This home, the Princeton Estate, had been the pastor's house. He was an abolitionist and had participated in the movement. Denise reached out to gently stroke the walls. She pressed the floor with her foot. The Princeton Estate had not only history but drama and character.

"This is the place, Sara. Perfect for your ceremony and reception." Denise ran her hand along the wall panel. "I feel it." She shared what she'd learned.

"I think you're right, soror." She squeezed her hand, a small giggle erupting. "Let's go sign the paperwork and write that big fat check."

"I don't think you'll be disappointed."

Witnessing Sara's excitement caught Denise unaware. All the wedding talk and visiting places drew her in, uncovering a whimsical desire to walk in Sara's shoes. More importantly, the planning made her think of Jaden.

Later that evening, Denise drove into the parking lot in front of Sara's apartment. The long day and full stomachs had worn them out. No one suggested that they stay for a nightcap. Denise was glad that she was exhausted because then she wouldn't focus on the fact that she hadn't talked to Jaden.

Sara hovered at the driver's door, shifting from one foot to the other.

"What's up, Sarafina? Something's on your mind." Denise turned off the engine. She didn't want her to feel rushed.

"Come up for a second."

Denise shoved the fatigue out of sight. Sara needed her. Hopefully she wouldn't be telling her some bad news about Jackson. Her line sisters had orchestrated a reunion once, and they'd do it again if they had to.

"You're making me scared." Denise closed Sara's door with her hips.

Sara laughed. "Relax. I know that I made it seem

ominous. Didn't mean to do that." She sat on the couch and patted the seat next to hers. Denise followed her direction, still a little uneasy.

"Remember our Hell Week, that last week of the pledge program?"

"Sure." Denise frowned, more curious.

"One of the assignments was to write a note to the line sister that you would entrust with your most precious request."

"Oh, yeah. That was a bit over the top. I can't even remember what I wrote. I think that I may have given mine to Athena." Denise laughed. "I must remember to ask her."

"I wrote in mine that, when I got married, I wanted you to be my maid of honor."

Denise hadn't remembered but was flattered into speechlessness. "I'm honored."

Sara took her hand. "You've done more for me than I could've expected."

"I'm shocked. Any of the other line sisters would work."

"I know, but I can only ask one person. And that person is you. We've seen a lot and shared a lot. I treasure our friendship and want to celebrate by making you my maid of honor."

"And I accept. Thank you for thinking about me." Denise hugged Sara.

Her soror was right. Many times through their pledge process when the Big Sisters had pushed at them with mind games and challenges, she had gotten through them with Sara at her side. Her positive approach to overcoming the hurdles had earned her a soft spot in her heart.

"I will tell the others individually," Sara said.

They were silent, just smiling at each other.

"I think that I'm on my way to becoming married. Can you believe that?" Sara whispered.

"I'm happy for you, but I must admit that it scares me a little."

"Me, too. But I want to hear why it scares you."

"It's all for selfish reasons. I'm used to picking up the phone and calling you or stopping by. I didn't have to consider someone else in your life. You were like my blood sister."

Sara placed a hand against hers. "Stop. Remember we always said that you don't need to be blood to feel that sisterly bond."

Denise nodded but she wasn't convinced that things wouldn't change. "If it means anything, I trust Jackson to take care of you."

"How old-fashioned of you. But I know what you mean. I need to relax around my in-laws. Don't want them to slip back into their old behavior."

"You have control, Sara. They treat you the way

you want to be treated. But this time around you changed the rules. And guess what? They couldn't do anything about it and risk losing Jackson, so they are sticking it out."

"Nothing can come between Jackson and me. Our previous separation helped to toughen our relationship. I love that man." Sara sighed. "Are there wedding bells in your future?"

"That's quite a leap from where we are now."

"It's not that complicated. Take my word for it."

"Jaden and I are...friends."

"Friends, as in a buddy or pal? Or friends, as in rolling-in-the-hay friends?"

"You and your crazy visuals. I don't know what we are but I really like him. But I don't think he's opened up to me."

"Have you trusted him with your information?"

Denise nodded.

"And still you doubt him?" Sara elbowed Denise in the arm. "Don't let something good get away."

"But I'm not even thinking of marriage now. I want to enjoy our friendship until it goes to that level."

"I guess I'm in my bride-to-be mode. Didn't mean to force you to the altar. But as a romantic at heart, I want to hope this is the man for you."

Denise nodded. To object would only motivate Sara to sink her teeth into her love life until she relented. The radiance emanating from Sara didn't hold guarantees for others.

"I'm going to get out of here. Thanks for the honor." Denise hugged Sara and then headed to her car.

In bed, she lay in the dark. Being surrounded by wedding themes and romantic clichés, Denise couldn't fight off her wandering imagination. The what-ifs added fuel to her doubts. She plumped her pillow with her fist.

She reached over for the phone and dialed.

"Jaden, it's Denise."

"Good to hear from you."

Denise dared hope that she heard pleasure in his voice. "I missed hearing from you."

"I've been so busy here. But I should wrap up everything by tomorrow. Then you can have me all to yourself." He chuckled. "I'm looking forward to that."

"Me, too." Denise searched for topics to discuss. When she was in his presence she could chat about things close to her heart. Over the phone, the flow was hampered. "How is your brother?"

"Why?"

"Nothing." She hesitated, shocked by his response. "I remembered that he was...ill when I last saw him."

"He's fine. Getting better. Maybe when you meet again you'll get a chance to talk."

"Right." Denise sensed an undercurrent of discomfort around the subject of Calvin. She'd only asked to be considerate. Maybe she'd try a different route. "I've been busy with Sara. Doing wedding stuff all day." She offered her news with the hope that he would follow suit. She didn't want to seem like she was prying.

"When is the wedding?"

"In three months. Not a lot of time. But they'd dated for a bit before their breakup and now that they are together again, they don't want to waste any more time."

"Better them than me."

Denise opened her mouth to share her news about being the maid of honor. But his unexpected remark unsettled her. Was he saying that he didn't want to be married? Or didn't want to be married to her?

"Hey, are you falling asleep on me?" he teased.

"No way. Marriage scares you?"

"Not at all. My parents have had a good marriage—I think. I don't believe that anyone should enter into it lightly."

Relief flooded Denise. "I agree. I'm open but not ready to jump the broom."

"Jump the broom?"

"You've never heard of that. Where have you been?"

"Excuse me, but that wasn't taught in my engineering classes."

"It's a custom that has its roots from the time of slavery when marriage ceremonies weren't allowed. A broom was used to symbolize sweeping the past and jumping into the future. Everyone at the wedding formed a community to witness the ritual and show their support."

"Sounds beautiful."

"Yeah. Don't know if Sara will do that. But I think that I'd like to do that." She bit her lip at her loose tongue. "Not that I'm making any hints."

"I don't listen to hints."

"Are you being deliberately difficult because I can't get my hands around your neck?"

"I don't want your hands around my neck. I have other places in mind."

"I'm here all alone. I'm wearing my two-piece lingerie. It's see-through. Blazing hot red."

"You are evil."

"Yes, I'm deliciously wicked." She moaned for his benefit. "But I don't want you to overdose on what could have been. I'll say good-night." She hung up the phone before he could respond. Then she turned off the phone. Quite satisfied with herself, she rolled over and welcomed sleep.

Jaden boarded the plane that would take him back home. The two days that he'd stayed in Florida had been emotionally draining. The path to this point had been bumpy and at times he wondered if getting Calvin into rehab would work.

Calvin had showed up at his house looking terrible, but sober. Jaden didn't have to talk him into getting on the plane. Wherever he'd been, he'd arrived at his house ready to go to rehab.

Now Jaden had to tell his parents. Calvin had offered to call them before he entered the facility, since calls to family were only allowed on certain days. Until he dealt with his family, he couldn't think about bringing Denise to meet his father or mother. He didn't need his parents to take a bite out of Denise because of their foul moods.

Choosing not to delay the news, he drove from the airport to his parents' place. Although he had made a bold move with his brother, his courage wiggled like a gelatin mold.

"Hi, Mom."

"Fancy seeing you here. Thought you'd have come this weekend. But never mind, I'm still glad to see you." She turned away from him and headed to the kitchen. "Have you had lunch? Looks like you lost weight."

"I haven't had anything since this morning, and that was a cup of coffee." Jaden walked farther into the house. "Where's Dad?"

"He's in his den." His mother leaned out of the kitchen area. "Grant? Jaden is here." She shook her head. "I never know what that man is doing. Grant!"

Jaden cringed when his mother roared in her high-pitched voice. He knew enough about his father to know that he'd come storming out of his den. Not exactly the mood he was after.

"I've got leftover tomato soup. You can have that with a grilled-cheese sandwich."

Jaden patted his stomach. "That'll work."

"What is all the commotion?" His father appeared wearing his usual scowl.

"Jaden popped in."

"Bring out the marching band." His father waved and turned to head back to his hiding place.

"Wait, Dad, it's about Calvin."

His mother banged the frying pan on the top of the range. She kept her back to him. But from the stiffness in her shoulders and stillness of her hands, he knew that she waited for his news. His father took a seat at the table. His eyes bored into Jaden.

"Calvin is no longer at the hospital," Jaden said.

"I know. We went to see him yesterday and they said that he'd checked out." His father's beefy hands were interlaced with each other. He zeroed in on Jaden.

"Calvin is in a rehabilitation center."

"Where?" his father asked.

"In Florida."

"You sent him to Florida," his mother's voice broke with anguish.

"He's there for ninety days. I checked out the place. I went there with him. He's happy. For the first time in a long time, he can relax and repair himself. He needs the separation from us."

"Why didn't you tell us before you did it?"

"Because I thought you would have tried to stop him." Jaden walked over to his mother, still bent over the range. Her shoulders shuddered and he knew that she was crying. "This wasn't meant to hurt you or cause any pain."

"He could have stayed here."

"I know, but I did what I thought was best." He gently took the bread loaf from her hands. "I'll make the sandwich. Go have a seat."

She sat next to her husband, but he was too absorbed in his thoughts to give her his attention. She played with her fingernails. "I know you had the best of intentions, Jaden. But to treat your brother like a..."

"An addict? He is an addict."

"Criminal. We are all addicts of something or the other. He hasn't hurt anyone."

"Yet." Jaden cut a small cube of butter and

allowed it to melt before swirling it around in the pan until the bottom was coated. He laid down the first slice, then the cheese and covered it with the other slice of bread. He held down the sandwich with the spatula. Only the soft sound of the sandwich cooking was heard.

His mother resumed her place in the kitchen and brought out the soup. She worked beside him but didn't say anything.

"Grant, set the table, please."

His father didn't move. Jaden wasn't sure that he'd heard his mother.

"Grant, set the table. We're ready to eat." His mother rarely used that authoritative voice. She had to be experiencing a strong emotion to get that no-nonsense attitude.

His father did set the table. But when they brought the food to the table, he stood. "I'm angry and I don't want to eat. I don't care how much it costs, I'm going to Florida tomorrow. Calvin is coming home with me and will stay here." His finger pointed down to the floor. His fury had surfaced now that reality had sunk in.

"Dad and Mom, I know you have trouble believing me. But I love Calvin just as much as you do. I'm not an evil person trying to have his brother institutionalized. Calvin understands the steps he has taken to get to this point. But now he's going to take the next steps with people who can help him. When he rejoins us, we will see how much he's grown. Grown as a man."

His father nodded. "How is he paying for it?"

"I'm paying for it."

"I'm sure we can help," his mother offered.

"I'll accept the offer."

"Let's hold hands and give thanks and praise." His father held his wife's hand and then offered his hand to Jaden.

As long as Jaden could remember, his father had never led a prayer. Maybe today was the beginning of many things. He longed for a new chapter with his family. Calvin wasn't the only one who would heal during the next three months.

Denise entered the family home, something she only managed to do when her father was at home. Otherwise, she'd meet her mother at a restaurant, or on the rare occasion in her own place. Her dad had returned from an overseas trip. She looked forward to hearing all about it.

Her mother and sister chatted on about nothing in particular. They both vied for her father's attention, updating him on every inch of their lives. Denise excused herself.

She took refuge in the bathroom, sitting on the

toilet seat. She'd been at her parents' house for over an hour discussing party details. Now she wanted to go, but Thea had manipulated her father into suggesting that they have a family dinner.

They didn't do family dinners. Denise always managed to be unavailable. Eventually they had stopped expecting her. Thea was being a real pain with family reconciliation. Knowing her, it was probably the topic on some show.

A knock on the door snapped her attention back to the present. She stood, straightened her clothes and flushed the toilet for good measure. After washing her hands, she opened the door to see her father scrutinizing her.

"All yours," she said.

"We're ready to eat."

Denise took her place at the table.

"Why the long face?" her father asked. "Thought you'd be happy to eat my cooking."

"You're cooking now?" Denise teased. She took a platter of rice pilaf from her dad.

"I know neither of you are going to eat until you've said grace." Her mother glared at them until they returned the serving dishes to the table and bowed their heads.

Denise waited for her mother to finish. Her mind closed out any words her mother uttered. Once she finished, she resumed the task of filling her plate with her father's cooking.

"I'm really looking forward to our party. Thank you, girls, for making it sound fabulous." Her mother's smile beamed on Thea and her. "I'd never thought to use the backyard for the cocktail reception."

"Saves us money. I'm all for that. Now, Thea, let's not go overboard on the guest list. I can feel a vacuum on the corner of my pocket," Denise grumbled.

"Nowadays, how often do people celebrate twenty years of marriage, of being in love with someone, of settling down with your soul mate?"

"Enough with the silly romantic crap." Denise couldn't help her eruption, blaming the dive in her mood to missing Jaden. "I've got to get home."

"I'm staying overnight. Why don't you?" Thea looked at her father, then her mother, for help.

Her mother kept her focus on her plate.

But her father was clearly angry with her. "Denise is free to go if she wishes. Never want her to feel like a prisoner in her home, or what was once her home."

"It's not that at all, Dad," she said. "I'm sorry." Denise would rather not stay after her bad behavior. The emotions that she'd tucked away and kept a tight lid on were pushing against her restraint. Lashing out at her mother came fast and, she had to admit, with increased intensity. She felt that the road of hidden hurt and suppressed anger may disappear under her feet. And she hadn't thought about the eventual blow-up that she felt building inside her.

"Maybe tomorrow we could go to church together." Thea continued to push her agenda.

"I didn't bring clothes."

"But I did and we still wear the same size."

Denise doubted her few extra pounds were shared by Thea, but she surrendered after seeing her father's disappointment.

Tonight promised to be long and agonizing.

After the house had settled, Denise lay in her bed in the room that she'd had as a child. It had become a place to store Christmas decorations. For the most part, the original setting remained, with the too-pink walls and frilly fabric.

"I was such a girly girl." She got up to open the drawers to her vanity. How many times had she sat at this mirror?

Her stomach growled. She'd skipped dessert, but a slice of pie would hit the spot now. She threw on her robe and quietly headed out of her room.

The entire house was blanketed in darkness. Thin slivers of light came from her parents' room and Thea's. She didn't want Thea's company on her snack run. Her over-the-top optimism might earn her a push down the stairs.

She eased down the stairs, carefully trying to remember which treads squeaked. Using her hands, she felt her way toward the kitchen.

Ten years ago she had done the same thing, sneaking out of her room to get ice cream.

Her father had been gone on business. She and Thea had been invited to a slumber party. But she had had no desire to hang out with Thea's friends, so she had come back home. Thinking that her mother was asleep, Denise had gone straight to the kitchen.

She had heard an upstairs door open and then someone had come down the stairs. Her mother's laughter had been loud and quite happy. Denise had hidden.

"You know you can't get away."

Denise had frozen. Someone else was in the house. Was her mother in danger? She hadn't known whether to jump out of her hiding place or slide into the pantry. But she had been afraid the door would make a sound. She had slid to the floor and remained as still as she could.

"I'll be right back. I have strawberries and whipped cream for us." Her mother had giggled like a schoolgirl.

"Screw the strawberries, but I could use the whipped cream." The man had laughed.

Denise had sat hunched on the floor, her mind whirring with confusion. Her mother hadn't sounded in danger. Yet that wasn't her father.

But it had sounded like him.

"I want to make love to you all over this house."

"No. And I'm not letting you into my bed. We agreed."

"You and your rules. How about the living room, then? My brother is a lucky man."

Denise had heard a roar in her head. She had clamped her hand over her mouth just in case the sound had come from her mouth. But it had been her body defending her from the acts of betrayal by her mother and her uncle. Her heart had been ripped in two. She had stayed there past his departure, her mother's return to the bedroom and the morning sun's appearance.

Now Denise wiped at the tears that could still pour at the memories of so long ago. She cut her slice of pie, opting to eat it at the kitchen counter. That night she had retreated into a web of secrecy.

Jaden went down to the hotel bar, hoping that a communal atmosphere while looking at the sports channel would take his mind off Denise. He couldn't be the only male in the hotel missing that special someone.

He entered the bar, immediately disappointed at the spattering of people. He took a seat at the counter.

"Good evening, sir. What can I get you tonight?" The bartender flipped a small towel over one shoulder and waited.

"Rum and cola."

"Coming right up." The bartender headed off to his rum supply.

Jaden took out his phone and set it on the bar. Then he put it back in his pocket. He didn't want to act like a lovesick wimp. "Man up," he muttered.

"Excuse me?"

A soft, lilting voice interrupted his solitude. Jaden turned to view its owner.

"Hi, I'm Celia." She outstretched her hand, which Jaden took. "May I join you?" The woman didn't wait for his response, slipping onto the bar stool next to him.

Jaden took his drink. He looked at the dark potent liquid.

"I'll have what he's having," she purred. "Here all alone?"

Jaden noticed the long, tanned legs, crossed in a sexy pose. The short skirt and silky top molded along her curvaceous body weren't lost on him. But he had no desire to play the game of flirtation.

Frankly, the hunger in her eyes irritated him, suggesting she was a regular in hotel bars wherever her business trips took her.

Finally, he answered, "No, I'm not alone. My wife is waiting for me. It was nice meeting you, Celia." He didn't bother to offer his hand. The brunette would have to toss her thick hair at someone who cared to appreciate the effort. Jaden picked up his drink, tossed down a couple bills and headed out of the bar.

Not that he considered himself a magnet to women, but he practically ran to his room to avoid any further meetings. Safe behind his hotel door, he climbed into bed and flipped open his phone.

"Hey, baby, I miss you." Jaden stacked the pillows and leaned back.

"I'm glad you called." He heard Denise sigh.

"What's wrong?"

"Nothing. I'm staying here at my parents'." She paused. "I'd rather be at home. You know how that goes."

"Yeah." Jaden didn't know what issues Denise had to deal with at home, but he could empathize from personal experience with his parents.

"I've been busy all of a sudden. With Sara's wedding coming at me so quickly, I hope that I can help her properly, as a maid of honor should."

"I'm sure you'll do fine. You said that she had a

planner. It's not as if you'd be doing the major logistical stuff that comes with holding a wedding."

"I've got to admit that I'm nervous for her."

"That's natural."

"Kind of. Well, you know how it is. I see people spend all this money and have dreams that are limitless. Yet, the split-then-blended family is on the rise." Her tone turned bitter. "Look at my family."

Jaden didn't know how to respond. He wanted to offer comforting words that could erase her low expectation.

"Let's not talk about this anymore. I sound like I need to talk to a shrink. Instead, I want to talk about you making love to me," she offered.

"I wish that I could do more than talk about it."

"Promise me that you will."

"Cross my heart, baby," Jaden stated.

Chapter 8

Jaden had tried the movies, an impromptu picnic and now a quiet stroll in the park to spark Denise to life. Her quietness and polite responses unnerved him. He stopped asking if he'd done something to offend her. But the heavy sighs and sad gazes stirred him into action to spend the day with her.

"You know, I missed you when I was gone."

"I missed you, too."

"Would you like to go off somewhere together?"

"Sounds wonderful."

Jaden guided her to a bench and took a seat. "I can't take it anymore. What did I do? Or what didn't

I do? You look sad. I'm not feeling sad. I didn't think
that I would make you this way."

She placed a hand on his cheek. "I'm really sorry.
It's not you." She kissed him. He wanted more but
recognized that she wanted to talk.

"I'm a good listener."

She nodded. Then kissed him harder. She
couldn't keep teasing him. He wasn't ashamed to
compare himself to a puppy who lost control with
a good belly rub.

He scooped her into his arms and returned her
kiss. He wanted to remove the pain that made her
wilt. In his arms, he wanted to protect her. His mouth
communicated its own message of hope and joy.

"You mean so much to me. I can't think straight
when I'm not around you. I crave your touch, your
laugh, your intelligence."

"Ditto."

They laughed at the famous line from one of her
favorite romantic movies.

"But seriously, I hate to see you worried. Is it
friends, family or me? Although, I don't want to
know if it's me. Allow me my illusions that we are a
fantastic couple enjoying each other's company."

"Friends are fine. I've been worried about us
moving on and drifting apart, but I'm realizing that
it's all part of growing up. Now that we're out of

college, the growing process has kicked into high gear. I get the feeling that Athena may be the first to leave and stretch her wings. That'll be a sad time."

He heard the quiver in her voice and pulled her close to him. Since he was the loner sort, he didn't have ties to friends that cut deeply. Leonard was his best friend. With a newborn, his life had taken a turn without Jaden.

"As for family…" Denise's laugh sounded tired and frustrated. "Families don't quite operate how you expect them to. I know there isn't any rule book. But there's got to be a code of honor somewhere. Don't you think?"

"I've wondered the same for a long time." He'd talked to Calvin once since he'd returned. The conversation hadn't gone well, as Calvin had reached a point when he had to open more of his soul to let in the therapists. Jaden had tried to talk him down from his panicked state. If Calvin were to show up at his front door, although he wouldn't be surprised, he'd be very disappointed.

"Would you take me to meet your family now?"

"As long as you don't think they are a reflection of me." He winked at her.

"One day, when you officially meet mine, I'll definitely make that statement."

"Let's go shock some old people." Jaden pulled

her up from the bench. "My mother will be thrilled
and embarrassed that she didn't get time to prepare
a feast for an army." Jaden drove to his parents' with
a lighter heart. He wasn't afraid for them to meet
Denise. She was a woman of substance who could
see past the imperfections of a family. The older he
got, the more he believed that there wasn't a family
without its cracks and fissures.

Jaden pulled up to the house. Now that he was
actually there, some of his bravado left. Her hand
slipped into his and they walked up to the front door,
comrades in arms.

Usually he used his key, but letting themselves
in would be even more of a shock. He knocked on
the door and waited. His father opened the door.
His surprise kept him rooted as his gaze shifted
from his son to Denise. Jaden cleared his throat
when he felt the gazing period had teetered over
into rudeness.

"Please come in."

"Denise, this is my father, Grant." He looked up
to see his mother approaching. "This is my mother,
Clarice. Mom, this is Denise."

Jaden relaxed when his mother threw her arms
around Denise and gave her a bear hug. And in a
flash, Denise had disappeared, locked into place by
his mother's arm. He offered a small wave and a mis-

chievous wink as she departed, which earned him her bared teeth.

"Now, that was a surprise." His father thumped him on his back. "Oh, no, you don't." His father pulled him by the elbow into another room. "You're coming with me and telling me all about this girl."

"I'm not telling anything because by the time we sit down for dinner, I'll have to rehash the same thing for Mom."

"Do you think that your mom isn't finding out the scoop from Denise? I like her look and vibe, but she's not strong enough to stand up to your mother's interrogation." His father shoved him down onto the sofa.

Jaden listed all the main details about when, where and how he'd met Denise.

"It makes sense now why you've been looking peaceful. That's what I call it, because I couldn't figure out the change in you."

"I'm far from peaceful, Dad. Too much stuff going on in my life."

"Yeah, but the other stuff has lost its priority with you. Now you have her at the top of your list. And I can see it. Heck, I agree with it."

A small knock on the door caught their attention.

"Come in," his father ordered.

"It's me. Um…it's your mother." Denise pointed with her thumb over her shoulder. "She's crying."

Jaden shot up from the sofa and hurried to the door. His father beat him there and they all hurried into the dining room, where his mother sat at the table.

She was drying her eyes, clearly startled to see them. She turned to Denise. "Which one came first?"

"Your husband."

"See, my Jaden is no longer a mama's boy. He's definitely all yours. You don't have to worry about a thing."

"What are you two talking about?" Jaden looked at Denise but she was giggling and his mother smiled sweetly at him and returned to work. "What just happened?"

"I think it was a test," his father said. "And you passed. Meanwhile, I'll quietly have a heart attack over yonder." He headed for the nearest chair and sat.

"I'm sorry, but your mother made me do it," Denise said.

"You can say no."

"Leave her alone," his dad chimed in. "I'm going to like getting to know Denise."

Jaden sat with his father at the dining table. Denise's first meeting went well. The empty place setting across from him was the only reminder that not all was perfect.

Denise couldn't deny that she was on high after meeting Jaden's parents yesterday. She'd settled comfortably into the family unit. Sitting across from Jaden, she'd felt the warm love of a strong family. She wanted to belong and share in that bond with the man she loved.

She knew in her heart that Jaden had strong feelings for her but didn't feel confident that those feelings translated into anything stronger.

With her own parents' anniversary four weeks away, Denise had to meet with Thea once more. This time Denise insisted on meeting at her own house. She had a lot of work to do and wasn't keen on driving any farther than necessary.

"We're here," Thea and her parents called as they walked through her door.

"Didn't expect to see all of you." Since reliving the dark moment, Denise had made any contact with her mother almost nonexistent.

"Well, I'm using this anniversary to celebrate Mom and Dad's marriage. But I think that it's also a perfect vehicle for all of us to bond."

Alarm bells clanged in Denise's mind. "We bond every time we meet for this party." She shook her head. No way was she going into a group therapy session with Thea.

"I thought you'd feel that way, so I invited therapist Sasha Luchenko to help us get under way. Mom and Dad are up for it. Now it's up to you."

Denise wondered if she had stepped into an alternate universe. Because if that was the case she wanted out right now. Thea couldn't really be serious. And this dark-haired, Eastern European woman looked as if she'd stepped off a runway in Milan.

This was it. Denise pushed up the sleeves of her blouse. "Are you sure you're up for a bloodbath?" Her response got the desired reaction of shock. "Tea, water, coffee? I may have a bottle of vodka if you want to make things more lively." The way she felt she might take a few shots.

"What's gotten into you? I barely recognize you." Her mother stood with her hands on her hips as Denise took drinking glasses from the shelf.

"Maybe being manipulated or blindsided by Thea's new-age stuff. Maybe it's having to deal with one more detail for this anniversary party. Maybe it's because I've had a long day and would like to relax with my man." With each statement she plunked a glass onto the counter.

"You're being deliberately vulgar."

"And you're so refined."

"What's that supposed to mean? I don't know what I've done to you, but you always treat me as if I'm your enemy."

Suddenly Denise couldn't remember what she was supposed to be getting to pour into the glasses. Tears blinded her. Anger choked her. She moved around the kitchen as if it were her first time, trying to give her body something to do before she screamed.

Her mother touched her shoulder and she flinched. "No. Don't do that. Why do you hate me?" her mother asked.

Denise saw Thea in the doorway. But it was too late—she couldn't hold back. "I don't hate you, as much as I try, because you're my mother. But I'll never forget what you did ten years ago. You stripped away my innocence."

"Denise, what are you saying?"

Thea entered but maintained her distance.

"Why don't you get your therapist in here for this session. It's about to be played and there won't be any repeat performances."

"Dad!" Thea shouted.

"I saw you, Mom. I saw Floyd. I came home from the slumber party."

"Oh, no." Her mother had the decency not to pretend that she didn't know what she referred to.

"Dad, what is she saying? Mom?" Thea screamed.

"Denise, it's okay." Her father took the glass out of her hand. He held her against his chest, stroking her hair. "It's okay. I know."

Denise tried to stop sniffling because she couldn't quite hear her father. She wished her heart wouldn't beat so loud. She wanted no one to move. "What did you say?"

"I know about your mother. She told me when you girls were in college. We went to counseling for it."

"That's why you don't want Floyd at the anniversary." Thea's cheeks shone with her tears.

Denise nodded. "Thea wanted to invite Floyd as a surprise for Dad so they could reconnect."

"No, I don't want him here." Her mother shook her head. "I wish that I could erase it all. I'm still working hard for your father's forgiveness and now for yours. I can't handle seeing Floyd."

"Would you all like to have a seat?" the therapist asked. "I think that you have managed to do my job for me."

Denise remained behind while everyone went to the living room. Now that she'd unburdened, she did feel lighter. But where to go from here? The stunning news that her father knew about his wife and brother's affair showed how much he wanted to keep his family together. He had hidden his pain well.

"I've tried to deal with your hurt and anger by buying you expensive gifts. Your own home. I didn't know what I'd done to earn your anger." Her mother stayed in the doorway. Growing up, she had seemed invincible and strong, full of feminist ideals. Now she appeared human, aging gracefully but vulnerable.

Denise didn't know how to respond.

"I want to be your friend again."

Denise tried to say the right words of hope, reconciliation and forgiveness. Her mouth wouldn't move. Her heart and brain warred between her intellectual stance and her purely emotional one. "I can't stay. I feel as if I'm going to suffocate." She ran past her mother, grabbed her car keys and headed for her car. She drove to Jaden's and jumped out. "Please be home." She sobbed hard as she banged on his door with her open hand.

She fell into his arms when he opened the door.

"Denise? What's the matter?"

She held his face and kissed him as if her life depended on it. If she held on to him like an anchor, she wouldn't get sucked away in the blackness of her feelings. Her world had shifted under her feet and she didn't like the feeling.

"Just hold me."

"I'm holding you."

"Don't let go."

"I won't."

There she stood until her heart calmed down. They hadn't moved from the doorway.

"Guess we make a sight."

"Doesn't matter. You're here." Jaden shut the door with his foot. "Whose butt do you want me to kick?"

Denise laughed. "I'm a little embarrassed at my theatrics, but I need to escape."

"From?"

"Family."

"Been there."

"But did you actually run crying from your house?"

"No, but I think you deserve to enter and exit with flamboyance." He stroked her head, pushing her hair from the side of face.

She could only nod as his tender ministrations stirred something on the opposite spectrum from anger and rage. His words were barely intelligible as she focused on how his mouth formed the words and his Adam's apple bobbed. She touched the thick, lean muscles of his neck leading up to his jaw. His jaw clenched and unclenched.

She kissed his neck, following the path that her fingers had just made. His hand cupped the back of her head as his mouth ravaged her with soft kisses.

He lifted her and headed up the stairs. She enjoyed being cradled against his chest. He placed her down onto his bed, but Denise didn't want to let go.

She pulled up his shirt, always looking forward to the view of his stomach muscles. Her fingers pressed along his muscles as if she were playing a piano, making him twitch. She grinned, letting her hands slide up the smooth wall of his chest muscles.

She peppered the area with kisses and soft strokes of her tongue.

He exhaled air with a loud hiss. He pulled off his shirt, providing her with better access. She showed her appreciation as she pulled him over her and wrapped her legs around his waist.

"Are you using me?" he whispered in her ear.

"Like a drug."

"What happens when you don't get the same effect?" He unsnapped her bra and tossed it aside. He kissed each breast, blowing on the tips of her nipples. "I'm not sure I can handle rejection." His tongue seared the tips before he covered each with his mouth.

Denise arched in the direction of his mouth. "Nothing about you will be rejected."

"Are you up for the test?"

She nodded. Then her hand stroked him. "I'd say that you are, too."

While she undressed, he readied himself with latex protection.

"You have to make love to me until I say stop." She lay back against the pillows, waiting to welcome him.

Jaden lowered himself, sliding into the warmth between her legs. He set the rhythm with long, slow strokes, coaxing her body's surrender. She wanted all of him. Subtly she raised her hips to ensure deeper pleasure.

His body slowly rubbing against hers flooded her entire being with sexual energy. There was no rush. No harried motion to get to an unknown place. Together they moved toward that peak that they had experienced as one.

His hands explored her body, grasping and releasing her hips.

"I'm ready," she moaned.

He grunted.

She shifted her hips and increased the motion, urging him to move toward the peak with every ounce of energy. They moved without pausing, holding on to each other, pushing forward, always forward to the point where all senses were on overload.

In a tangle of arms and legs, with her throat parched, eyes closed against any light, she leapt into the abyss as her body spasmed along with Jaden's in a tingling plummet.

There they fell until they landed in reality on the bed. Denise held on to Jaden until she trusted herself to let go.

As much as she wanted to, Denise didn't stay at Jaden's for the night. She had run from her feelings. Even after Jaden had made love to her, she couldn't pretend that the previous events of the tumultuous evening hadn't occurred.

She entered her house. A lone light was on in the family room. A note was stuck on the refrigerator. She pulled it from the magnet and read it.

Sis, call me when you're ready.

A noise behind her startled her.

"Thea, what are you doing here?"

"I wrote the note, then decided to hang around. I fell asleep on the sofa." She yawned and stretched. "Do you have anything to drink?"

"Root beer should be in the fridge. Help yourself." Tension pooled in her body. She felt herself go on guard.

Thea opened the fridge and pulled out a can. "Want one?"

"Sure." Denise took it from her and headed to the family room. She took a seat and waited for Thea to follow.

"Why didn't you ever tell me?"

"How could I tell you? I couldn't grasp what I'd seen and certainly didn't want to deal with it afterward. Even now, with all the revelations of today, I can't give you a rational thought on all of this."

Thea pulled up her knees and rested her chin. "Mom was pretty upset."

Denise picked at her nails. "Did Dad stay with her?"

"Yes, he gave her a sedative and then they left.

Actually, Sasha was able to calm her. But I know that your witnessing everything hit her."

"Do you forgive her?" Denise didn't care if her question was fair.

"I'm shocked and hurt. But I think that seeing her hurt and Dad holding her in his arms and his face full of pain, I can't turn my back on her." Thea wiped away a tear.

"I wasn't asking you to do that." Denise was irritated that Thea could go on as if nothing had happened. Yet she understood what her sister had said.

"Are you willing to meet with Sasha?"

"I'm not the one with issues."

"But maybe your other problem, the gambling, could be resolved."

"Back off, Thea." Denise hated anyone focusing attention on her problem. She wished she could bury her head and not have to deal with that burden around her neck.

Thea unfolded her legs and stood. "I'm going to head home now. But I want to give you Sasha's number. If you call her, great. If you don't, it's your call." She walked over and hugged Denise.

Denise hugged her back.

"I want to celebrate the anniversary no matter what." Thea looked at her. Her younger sister, whom she had casually dismissed so many times before, now showed an inner strength. She was willing to challenge her for something she believed in.

"I agree."

"However, I will honor your request to leave Uncle Floyd out of it. I know that Mom isn't ready to see him."

Denise nodded. She didn't have Thea's sweet nature to allow Floyd back into her life.

"Sis, I love you." Thea grabbed her by her arms and gently shook her. "I've always looked up to you. And I will continue to do so."

Denise lowered her head onto her chest. Her sobs came out muted. "I love you, too, li'l sis."

Chapter 9

Denise sat in the therapist's office, questioning the step she was about to make. She'd never followed Thea's advice on anything. But remaining stuck with her anger and hurt didn't make sense. Feeling vulnerable scared her, but she didn't want to be a coward. Not anymore.

The therapist welcomed her, giving her the time needed to get comfortable. She asked many preliminary questions that Denise expected. At first, Denise tried to analyze the reason for the questions, but Sasha didn't reveal any significant emotion over Denise's one-word answers or her detailed explanations.

"Your resistance is pretty strong." Sasha's strong accent distracted her.

Her therapist belonged in a movie with Ingrid Bergman or with her daughter, Isabella Rossellini. Denise hoped that she hadn't bought into the Hollywood mindset that everyone needed a therapist. The trend was expensive and fairly intrusive. Sasha's sculpted face, long black hair—possibly a weave—and kick-ass olive tan advertised the benefits of listening to neurotic people.

"I shouldn't be so cynical about this. Guess I'm here for miracles. But I'll settle for a character makeover." Denise sat in a comfortable chair, glad to see that the classic, typical couch was nowhere in sight.

"I don't make things happen unless you want them to occur. I guide you, showing you options, warning you of the pitfalls, maybe revealing choices that you'd never considered." Sasha opened her black book and waited with pen poised over the blank page. Her round eyes, vivid blue, blinked with an owl-like wisdom. "Tell me what is holding you back? Real or perceived."

Denise took a deep breath. "I'm a gambler. Yet I haven't had the urge to play with chance nor have I thrown away hard-earned money for a long time. But usually something stressful triggers the urge." She

told Sasha about the last public humiliation. "Jaden
came along and took me out of there before I made
a bigger fool of myself." Denise's face warmed with
embarrassment. Jaden may have brushed off her
behavior, but the humiliation still resonated.

"Jaden is your boyfriend?"

"Jaden is one of the reasons that I'm here. I'm
unable to return his feelings. Well, not unable, but
scared. This fear is crippling me. I can't be this
broken person for him to fix. I want to be whole."

"Perfection is noble."

"But not realistic, I know. I want to commit to
him, but I'm afraid that I won't live up to it." She
pinched the bridge of her nose. "My mother certainly
didn't." Her teeth clenched after the angry statement.

"And there's the root that has colored your outlook."

Denise nodded. The root in her life had turned ugly
and rotten. Instead of inspiring and nourishing whatever
emotions grew within her, this foreign body corrupted.

"You expected perfection from your mother. You
expect it from your father, stepfather and even Thea.
But your mother tumbled off that pedestal. Right
now, she's not trying to climb back on. She wants to
meet you eye to eye."

"She lied." Denise glared at Sasha, as if she didn't
understand. "She took away something that should
be natural between mother and daughter. I want

things to be normal again. I really do. But when I see her, I see that night." She closed her eyes to tell her story but quickly reopened them to avoid the mental picture. "Floyd, my stepfather's brother, is nothing to me. And that won't change."

"And I can't erase your memory. Nor can you go back to the way things were. You tell her how you feel. You write how you feel. But at some point you have to turn the page and agree not to reach back and pull the anger and hurt from the past. Or you will be stuck. You will become bitter. You will use it as an excuse to keep your heart closed. Closed not only to her, but to everyone around you. Even Jaden."

Sasha's words and meaning scared her.

"And you've got to be prepared to put in the time to heal and even reprogram your brain, like judging, prioritizing, understanding your worth."

"I know." Denise refrained from telling her that she wanted the express version of therapy. Her time to rehabilitate to deal with the next phase of her relationship with Jaden was almost upon her. She didn't know if she had the courage to take that chance.

Jaden pulled up in front of his parents' house. He hadn't called ahead, and he hoped that they would be home. Nothing like a summer rain shower to accentuate the possible outcome of this trip home. He shut off the wipers, and within seconds the deluge of water blurred his windshield. Lights were on in the house, but he couldn't discern if his father came to the window to investigate the noise of the car.

"Where's Mom?" he asked his father when he entered the house.

"She's out on the back porch, repotting several plants."

"Tell her to come in. I've got a surprise for you both."

His father's expression changed, looking wary, before he headed off to get his wife.

Jaden made sure that his father had gone through the house before signaling back to his car. Calvin ran through the rain, ineffectively holding a newspaper over his head. They both had to flick off the water since they hadn't bothered to use umbrellas. Jaden heard his parents' approaching footsteps. He stepped aside.

"Surprise!"

Calvin stepped in between Jaden and his parents with outstretched arms. Jaden had to admit that his brother looked one hundred percent better. The pallor of alcoholism had vanished. His frame was still too thin, but he didn't look as if he was being consumed from within. Despite the sharp contours of his face, his younger brother had resumed some measure of his attractiveness.

"Calvin." His mother hugged him. She repeated his name, touching his face, as if she couldn't believe that he was in her house. "Let's go to the kitchen."

"Good to see you, son." His father also took his turn to hug Calvin. The old man's lips disappeared as he bit down, struggling to keep emotions in check.

His mother kept patting her heart. "Are you here for a while?"

"Yes and no, Mom. I'm done with my program. I still have to go to weekly meetings because the demons aren't completely gone. I know that I have a sickness that is with me for life." Calvin paused and looked over to Jaden.

Jaden gave him the thumbs-up, knowing that what his brother would reveal might not be met with enthusiastic support. As a matter of fact, he expected a fight.

Calvin, with his hands stuck in his pockets, shoulders hunched, continued, "I have a couple great job offers in Florida. I'm considering them."

"Oh, no." His mother froze. "You can't think about leaving us. You just got back." Jaden reached out for his mother, but she squirmed away.

"You knew this. Calvin needs to be home." She shook her head, looking defeated. "You knew this and didn't tell me."

Jaden didn't mind the dramatics. He was used to his mother doing whatever necessary to motivate any one of the men in the house to do what she wanted. But this time, she seemed older, a little more bent over, a little slower in her walk. She wasn't the little ball of energy that he was accustomed to and had taken for granted. He signaled to Calvin to continue.

"I interviewed to be an assistant football coach for an after-school program. I've found an apartment. You know, it's time for me to be on my own and do some growing up. I like living out there, not under anyone's shadow." He raised his hands. "No offense."

"None taken." Their father hugged his son.

Jaden relaxed and hoped that his parents would also follow suit.

"I'm glad to see that you've got a plan. When do you start?" his father asked.

"Next Monday."

"That means you're only here for four days," their mother wailed, but a stern look from their father and she suppressed any further protest. "Well, I'm going to cook some food and put it in containers so you can have home-cooked food. You look a little skinny."

Everyone laughed, a release from the tension that had formed like a thundercloud to match the weather.

Jaden looked at Calvin, happy for the temporary respite to victory. His mother, busy with her new tasks, had the opportunity to feel needed. His father had glimpses of the old Calvin as they retreated to

the den to catch up. Jaden knew better than to think
the storm had run its course. The chance of relapse
was strong in this early stage, when stress could
trigger his craving. Florida, he hoped, would reveal
its fountain of youth to his little brother, Calvin.

After dinner and more conversation, Jaden readied
to leave. The farewell turned into crying, hearty
good-luck statements and a large measure of hope.

Jaden followed Calvin to the car. Calvin used to be
the one to follow in Jaden's footsteps. He had marched
forward, taking it for granted that Calvin would keep
up. Now, as his brother walked with an air of uncer-
tainty, Jaden found himself with the now-natural
tendency to stay close behind him, prepared for the fall.

They exchanged eye contact before Calvin got in
the car. Warts and all, this was his brother. He found
himself hanging on to hope.

"Jaden." His mother had followed him outside.

He walked over to her standing on the porch.

"You continue to make me proud. This is the best
gift you gave me."

He touched his chest, thrilled that she appreciated
his small effort.

"But you don't look quite happy."

He shrugged. The days for crawling onto his

mother's lap and unloading his problems were long over.

His mother took a deep breath. "It's your woman? Denise? Sometimes everything can be going in the right direction, but if matters of the heart don't move the way we want, then it can feel as if your whole world is tilted." She hooked her arm through his and walked toward his car.

"I want to tell her that I love her."

"And...?"

"I'm afraid that she won't respond."

"Do you need her words? Have her actions not shown you the truth?"

He shrugged. "I'm not a mind reader."

"That's not what I asked you." She laughed. "Son, not everyone communicates in the same way. Some use words, some use art, some use symbols, some use their actions."

"Action is her thing."

"What has she done that made you love this woman?"

Jaden thought about the first time that he'd seen her. He'd admired her on that first day when she was stepping. "She's a beautiful woman. She's a thoughtful one when she helped me deal with Calvin and one of his episodes. She enjoyed meeting the family, practically insisting that we should do so to take our relationship to the next level. She's funny and spicy and loyal…"

"See! These are not the actions of a woman who only wants to be friends. What you want to demand from her may be too difficult for her to say with the same ease that you do."

Jaden kissed his mother's cheek. Guess he wasn't too old for his mother to heal any hurt and send him on his way. He'd stay out of Denise's way until Sara's wedding.

Sara's wedding day had perfect weather. The sun rose high into a cloudless sky. A gentle breeze blew through, chasing away any signs of humidity. Everywhere the landscape had verdant shades of green or splashes of bright color from the wildflowers in full bloom. Nature seemed to have joined in the celebration.

Denise couldn't agree more.

By midmorning, she and her sorors who were also part of the wedding party followed explicit instructions and headed for the church. They sat quietly in the limo, each woman lost in her own thoughts.

"I hope this doesn't change things too much." Asia looked out the window, but her faraway expression revealed that she was not paying attention to the immediate scenery.

"You know it will or else you wouldn't have to mention the possibility," Denise responded. The thought had not only crossed her mind, but nestled with a certain unease that accompanied change.

"Oh, please, let's not get all dramatic and deep. This is Sara's day. I don't want to hear about anyone's hang-ups." Naomi looked pointedly at Denise. Even she had been transformed from a tomboy to an elegant woman.

"Since I'm a lover, not a fighter, I'd like to say that we look darn good." Athena took out her compact and dabbed at her nose. She shrugged before snapping it closed. Nothing needed to be done. Her makeup was flawless.

They'd dressed in the hotel suite that Sara had reserved for them. Makeup artists had arrived with single-minded focus to get them ready for their bridesmaid roles.

The limo pulled up in front of the church, whose gothic design added a touch of Old World. Sara had wanted the most romantic wedding possible. Denise, however, hoped the strapless gowns would not be frowned on by the congregation or clergy. Maybe the modern style caused Sara to pick simple accessories and hairstyles.

"Ladies, we're not the bride. Put down the compacts. You look stunning, and if I were a man, I'd be stumbling over my feet to help you." Denise gently pushed Asia toward the door, where the driver patiently waited.

"That's a scary thought," Naomi teased.

They emerged from the limo in a soft rainbow of colors. Each woman stood side by side, adjusting her dress, fussing over the small details on each other.

Pastels were the color of choice. Each dress represented a shade of soft pink, blue, green, coral. Denise had chosen the coral color since it was the most difficult shade to wear without the right skin tone. It looked lovely on her.

"Let's go in." Denise took the lead.

Passersby, along with wedding guests, stopped to admire them. Their presence caused a stir, raising the level of anticipation for the bride's arrival. Denise didn't see the limo that Sara would use. But she had no doubt that her soror would not be late for her wedding.

The wedding planner spotted them. She hurried over to them, waving her hands. The women giggled at her harried state, but she was dressed like a million dollars.

"Please, ladies, Sara is in the vicinity. I need you to come into this waiting room. It won't be long, but I want to get people seated as soon as possible."

"I can't wait to see her," Asia remarked, as she was gently pushed into the room by the planner.

"Did anyone finally get to see the dress?" Naomi asked.

Everyone shook their heads.

"Knowing Sara, it's going to be nothing short of gorgeous." Asia sighed and dabbed at her eye.

"Oh, no, you don't." Denise stepped up and pinched her arm.

"Ouch! What is your problem?" Asia rubbed her arm. Any tears that had shown up had now fled.

"You can cry to your heart's content after the wedding, or at least after we get down the aisle. We all know that you can't stop crying once you've started," Denise scolded.

"Shh." Athena peeked out the door. "She's here." She gasped.

The others ran to the door for their view of Sara's entrance. Denise didn't appreciate having to stand behind Naomi, who didn't have to tiptoe. She elbowed her way to the door.

"She'll need help with that train." Denise stepped out of the room, but the planner beat her to Sara's side.

Just then, Sara looked up. Her face broke into her familiar grin. She reached out her gloved hand and Denise stepped forward to squeeze. They air-kissed, while a burst of giggles erupted between them.

"You look marvelous," Denise said. The emotion welled in her. After the hard time she'd given Asia, she couldn't possibly cry.

Her soror looked like a fairy-tale princess in crisp

white satin that framed her in a narrow, straight line. The style was reminiscent of the late '50s, as modeled by Audrey Hepburn in her movies. The tiny waistline sported a sequined band.

The top half had a delicate lace overlay with tiny sequins that glinted under the sunlight. The spaghetti straps showed off her skin, which had been dusted with a shimmering powder. She looked as if she'd been sprinkled with fairy dust.

The bottom half narrowed to her feet. Although it didn't have the intricate work of the top, the familiar glint of sequins was interspersed in the skirt. Tiny ballerina-style shoes peeked from the hemline.

"This is your day, sweetie," Denise declared.

"My heart feels like it's going to burst." Sara did sound breathless. The bouquet shook as she held it in front of her. The selection of flowers matched the pastel colors of their dresses.

"We've got to get started." The wedding planner didn't wait for them to agree or disagree. She motioned to the rest of the group to fall into place. Like someone who had a little too much caffeine, she buzzed around them, fixing and straightening, then stepping back to survey her handiwork, before moving in to fix again. "Fantastic!" She threw up her hands with a look of pure joy. "We will begin." Off she hurried, disappearing into the church.

"My stomach is in knots. My knees are shaking."
Sara walked toward the door to take her place. She
turned around. "Is Jackson here?"

"Of course. You know your line sisters wouldn't
let anything crazy happen on your day."

Sara bit her lip. "As we know, I've been here before."

Naomi marched to Sara's side. "You are not going
to think about that nimrod. You didn't marry him, so
that doesn't count. Your true love is waiting in there."
She softly touched Sara's cheek. "And you don't
want us to drag you in there, right?"

Sara grinned. "Not on your life. Denise, help me
with my veil."

Denise fixed the headpiece, lowering the veil into
place. "You're going to have to let me get a photo of
you." She hurriedly pulled out her digital camera and
snapped a couple shots, much to the planner's
dismay. "Let's go do this."

The wedding ceremony had enough reverence,
humor and tears to make it a worthy memory. Flowers and satin bows decorated the chapel, marking the
type of festivity unfolding under the cathedral ceiling. No sounds of children crying pierced the air.
Only an occasional, subdued cough interrupted the
solemn state.

From her position next to Sara, Denise viewed the

men in their slate-gray tuxedoes and matching bow ties. Jackson's groomsmen represented a diverse sampling of ethnicities who came to share on his day. She glanced out to the attendees, searching through the heads until she found Jaden. He raised his finger to his lips and furtively blew her a kiss. Her wink acknowledged her receipt. Later she would only settle for the real thing.

The vows were the couple's creation. Denise listened to sincerity that rang through the words of conviction and pure love. In this official and religious commitment ceremony, their love surrounded them in a warm cocoon. But Denise suspected that their cocoon had the strength of steel.

A tear slipped out and she quickly dabbed. Over her tissue, she caught Asia's eyes, which had started their own leaking. Subtly tissues were distributed along the bridesmaids' line to stem the steady stream.

Once more, Denise glanced over to Jaden. Standing as a witness to love did something to her head. Her heart had already gone to the other side, but her head, her mind was slow to follow. Looking at Jaden, her man—strong, compassionate, loyal and fearless—she couldn't imagine her life without him. She was glad he had agreed to come to the wedding. Most guys felt too much pressure with the occasion.

Her attention returned to the ceremony for the exchange of rings and the kiss, which caused an eruption of cheers and applause. As the final act of the ceremony, Sara and Jackson jumped over the broom together to the congregation's riotous delight.

Denise endured the receiving line and the long photo session. Part of her impatience was due to being unable to get to Jaden. The wedding planner guarded them with the zeal of a prison guard. They couldn't go to the ladies' room without her permission with strict instructions to return in two minutes.

Denise decided that two minutes was better than nothing. She made sure to walk close to the church's entry, where Jaden waited.

"Are you bored out of your mind?" Denise bumped him with her knee.

"Nope. I'm enjoying this actually. I think you look sexy in that dress."

"Shh. You're in a church. You can't use that word or have those thoughts."

Jaden grinned up at her. "What I plan to do won't be near any church." He moved his leg to avoid her playful slap. "There's a woman glaring at us."

Denise didn't want to turn, but she didn't have to. The planner stood at her side. "I think you're needed elsewhere." Her tone froze any further flirtatious moments Denise thought of entertaining.

Denise headed back with the planner's hand securely attached to her wrist.

The reception provided a wonderful wrap-up for the wedding celebration. The weather continued to grace the proceedings as the afternoon wound down. The country manor was a hit. The guests admired the setting with many compliments. The planner had outdone herself with an intimate romantic setting of cream with splashes of the pastel colors along the tables and decorations. No one had to tell her that she'd done a good job. Her self-evaluation was evident in how she strutted around the reception. She'd also managed to soften her directives toward the bridesmaids, as Denise pointed out to keep Naomi from clobbering the woman.

With military precision, the introduction of the wedding party and of the newly married couple signaled the beginning of the reception. Denise had barely had time to eat when Sara and Jackson were told to begin the first dance. In a matter of minutes, every bridesmaid and groomsman joined the couple in a waltz around the floor. Denise made small talk with her escort to be polite. Once the dance was over, she thanked him and went in search of Jaden. He was in deep conversation with the men at his table, talking about sports.

She leaned into his ear. "I want to dance with

you." She gently blew in his ear, just in case he thought he could finish his thought on this year's draft pick for pro football.

Jaden excused himself and took her to the dance floor. "You like to play dangerously, I see." He pulled her close to him. "You know, I just realized that we've never danced with each other."

"We've danced, maybe not on a dance floor. But what we've done is no different." She slid her hips against his, maintaining eye contact for her silent message. A seductive love song played in the background.

"Hmm. You do have some rhythm." At that moment, he spun her around, bringing her back to face him.

"I was thinking the same thing of you. I can't have a boyfriend who can't keep a beat." Denise subtly rubbed her body against his before resting her head against his chest.

"Do you dare doubt my skills?"

"No, it's just been a while since I got to see or feel them. I might be out of practice by the time you next exercise your skills on me."

Jaden kissed the top of her head. "I could eat you up, right now."

"Promises. Promises."

Jaden dipped her. His eyes slid down to her mouth. Then he righted her and pressed his lips against her temple. Jaden deftly spun her, breaking away from further skin contact.

They finished the song in a tight embrace. Denise closed her eyes, swaying to the beat. The next song began and they hadn't released each other.

"Denise," Jaden said softly.

"Yes."

"I love you."

Denise's feet remained rooted, abruptly interrupting their dance. She'd wanted to hear those words.

"I love you." Jaden repeated against her hair. She pressed her head against his chest.

She couldn't budge, despite the subtle pressure to continue the dance. Jaden took a step back from her. She dared not look into his eyes. Her pulse had picked up speed.

"Did I say something wrong?" Jaden asked, slowly.

"No," she whispered. The hurt in his tone gripped her heart. "Thank you."

"What does that mean? I don't want your gratitude. I want to hear you say that you love me. I thought that you loved me."

"This isn't the time or place." Denise looked around to make sure no one had picked up on their disagreement. "I've got to go."

"Once again, you're on the run." He matched the pace of her retreat. "This time, we're going to talk this one through." He held on to her elbow. "What games are you playing?"

She'd almost reached the door. "I can't think." She shook her head. "I'm not ready." Suddenly, the hairpins stuck in her hair to keep up the style bothered her. The dress, with its layers of lace, itched her skin. Her feet grew tired of the pumps. She wanted out of everything.

"Love isn't on a schedule. There's no appointment on a calendar. It just happens." Jaden stepped between her and the door. "What are you afraid of?"

Denise stepped back. Her eyes welled with tears. "I want you with all my heart."

"Okay. I can live with that." He rubbed his forehead.

"But shouldn't have to."

"If you can't say that you love me, then tell me that you don't love me. Tell me that it's over."

"You caught me off guard. The wedding was beautiful. Sara and Jackson, they bring tears to my eyes." She gulped. "My life is on the mend. I'm a little broken. I want to come to you when I'm whole, in one piece, telling you that I'm ready. You don't deserve any less. I'm not your responsibility to fix. What if I can't kick my habit? What if I let you down, or bring you down?"

Jaden stepped aside, allowing her to pass. His gaze was fastened on a distant point. His mother's advice seemed a long time ago. Pretending that he didn't need to hear her response only worked for so long.

Denise found the bridal suite reserved for Sara if she needed to get away or to change. During her hasty, teary-eyed exit, she'd bumped into Sara. Blurting Jaden's name earned her the key with no questions asked. Denise appreciated that Sara didn't follow.

A knock sounded on the door.

Curiosity must have got the best of Sara. Now she'd play mother hen at her own wedding. Denise could suck it up long enough to tell Sara to ignore her meltdown.

She opened the door, expecting to see Sara. Instead, Athena stood barefoot in the doorway with her shoes in one hand and a glass of water in the other.

"Sara sent me. Actually she commanded. So talk!" Athena handed the glass to Denise.

"I screwed up. Big." Denise spun the water glass around in her hand.

"I'm listening."

Denise filled her in, which meant that she had to disclose her family's issue, more about her gambling addiction and her fear of depending on Jaden for all the wrong reasons.

Athena clucked her tongue. "That's a heck of a lot to deal with. I'm sorry that you felt you had to carry

that load. And what about Jaden? Did he run for the
hills when you told him all this?"

Denise shook her head. She squirmed.

"Don't tell me, you haven't told him anything."
Athena leaned back in the chair and glared.

"I don't want to lose Jaden."

"Unless you prepare to commit, you will lose him.
You're doing all the right things to get you to the right
place. Having a supportive, loving man at your side
is a bonus."

"My love life is a shambles. My relationship with
my mother is a shambles."

"Sounds like you need to get off the high horse
and be among us little people." Athena pulled out her
compact and repaired the damage in Denise's makeup. "I know Sara was the one to tell it to you like it
is. And I'm willing to use it to knock some sense into
you." With one hand resting on her hip, she jabbed
at the air between herself and Denise. The shoes
looked as if they would fly and knock Denise in the
forehead. Denise leaned back just in case. "Your
mother has apologized. She has tried to make up for
what she's done wrong. I'm not saying you can't be
hurt, but you also can't let it act like battery acid on
your relationship. And Jaden sounds like the perfect
man for you. I'm not sure anyone else can put up with
your self-centered attitude. You said he's got prob-

lems with his brother. I think that makes him qualified to handle your crazy behind."

"My therapist doesn't abuse me the way you do." Denise's face burned with humiliation and the truth that Athena had turned a spotlight on.

"I'm also not getting paid."

It was as if a lightbulb had gone on in her head. Denise shot off the chair. "Do you think he left?"

"I would have. But I think one of those skeezers may have their hooks in him by now. There is a shortage of men at this party. Look for a big booty girl with a red hair weave. I think she's the one he was dancing with."

Denise left Athena and ran to the reception room. Some of the guests had left, while others clustered in small groups, chatting. No one was left on the dance floor.

She scanned the room looking for Jaden or Miss Red Hair. No sign of either. She headed for the door when a hand closed around her wrist and pulled her down.

"What the—" She landed in Jaden's lap and spontaneously hugged him. In his embrace, she stayed there, grateful that he'd remained.

"Jaden Bond." Denise snuggled against his cheek.

"Yes, Denise Dixon."

"Will you be my soul mate?"

"Forever."

"Will you love me?" She kissed the side of his sexy mouth.

"Forever."

"No matter what issues I've got in my life—and I am working on them—I'd rather have you in my life than out of it."

"I'm here for you, Denise, just as I know you'll be there for me. Through whatever."

She hugged him close. "You got that right."

Epilogue

Denise ticked off the many events that required her presence. The last in the lineup of events was her parents' wedding anniversary party. She'd taken time off from work and stayed hidden in her house. No one bothered her, sensing that she needed the retreat.

Tonight, under the bright lights of the event, it was her first venture out with the family. She didn't feel any sense of dread. Her mother looked stunning, and her father had lost years off his appearance as he greeted the many guests.

More importantly, Jaden stood at her side.

"You're looking fabulous," he whispered. "Don't worry."

"Jaden, good to see you," her mother said, kissing

each on the cheek. "I've enjoyed chatting with you, Jaden. Take care of my daughter. She means everything to me."

Jaden had insisted that he meet her parents again.

Denise walked up to her mother and hugged her, long and hard.

"You've got a great man. I'm proud of you." She paused. "I'm so sorry, sweetheart," her mother whispered in her ear.

Denise tried to talk, but the tears flowed. She still hadn't released her mother, when her sister popped her head into view.

"Everyone's staring. You're going to have to go blubber somewhere else," Thea interrupted.

Denise smiled. Yep, her sister would make a good socialite—and there was nothing wrong with that. Denise took a deep breath, cleansing the worry, fear and insecurity from her system. Jaden stood at her side, his strong hand clasped in hers. His love had the power to be a physical cloak that covered and protected her. Leaning against his body, she looked forward to being a wife to this man and a mother to their children.

"When can we blow this joint?" he whispered. "I want to make you holler tonight."

"Behave," she scolded, but the mischievous giggle that erupted said otherwise.

Slowly they eased out of the party and headed for the car.

Tyson Braddock was not a man to be denied....

Second Chance, Baby

Book #3 in The Braddocks: Secret Son

A.C. ARTHUR

Except for one passion-filled night, Ty and Felicia Braddock's
marriage has been cold for years. Now Felicia is pregnant.
Unwilling to raise her baby with an absentee workaholic
father, Felicia wants a divorce. Ty convinces her to give him
another chance. But as they rediscover the passion they'd lost,
will it be enough to make them a family?

THE BRADDOCKS

SECRET SON

power, passion and politics are all in the family

Available the first week of October wherever books are sold.

Will being Cinderella for a month
lead to happily ever after?

A Gentleman's Offer

DARA GIRARD

Wealthy Nate Blackwell offers dog groomer Yvette Coulier
an opportunity to live among the upper crust if she'll let him
pose as her valet. But it's not long before their mutual passion
forces them to take off their masks...and expose their hearts.

BLACK STOCKINGS SOCIETY

Four women. One club.
And a secret that will make all their fantasies come true.

Available the first week of October wherever books are sold.

KIMANI
ROMANCE™

www.kimanipress.com

KPDG085i008

She was beautiful, bitter and bent on revenge!

Tender SECRETS

ANN CHRISTOPHER

Vivica Jackson has vowed vengeance on the wealthy
Warners for causing her family's ruin—but that's before
she experiences Andrew Warner's devastating charm.
After the would-be enemies share a night of fiery passion,
each is left wanting more. But will her undercover
deception and his dark family secret lead to a not-so-
happy ending to their love story?

"An exceptional story!"
—*Romantic Times BOOKreviews*
on *Just About Sex*

Available the first week of October wherever books are sold.

KIMANI™
ROMANCE

www.kimanipress.com   KPAC0871008

What Matters Most

ESSENCE BESTSELLING AUTHOR
GWYNNE FORSTER

Melanie Sparks's job at Dr. Jack Ferguson's clinic is an opportunity to make her dream of nursing a reality—but only if she can keep her mind off trying to seduce the dreamy doc. Jack's prominent family expects him to choose a wealthy wife. But he soon realizes he's fallen for the woman right in front of him.... Now he just has to convince Melanie of that.

*Coming the first week of October
wherever books are sold.*

ARABESQUE®

www.kimanipress.com

KPSKI040908C